BEYOND BUDAPEST

by

J. D. MALLINSON

Inspector Mason novels:-

Danube Stations
The File on John Ormond
The Italy Conspiracy
The Swiss Connection
Quote for a Killer
Death by Dinosaur
The Chinese Zodiac Mystery
A Timeshare in France

WAXWING BOOKS, NEW HAMPSHIRE

CHAPTER ONE

The express double-decker bus sped, with an occasional stop to pick up passengers, through the dormitory communities north of Manchester. It then commenced the steady climb up the twisting moorland road towards the village of Balderstones nestling in the valley of the River Tame on the western flank of the Pennines, the chain of limestone hills that formed the backbone of England from the Peak District to the Scottish border. Inspector George Mason, sitting on the upper deck, had ample time to take in a view of rolling moorland divided for the most part by dry-stone walls forming enclosed pasture for sheep grazing the steep hillsides. It was a stirring sight on this late-summer day, even though weeks of drought had produced large areas of a rusty brown color marring the normal dark-green of the open moors, broken only by crumbling walls and a few wind-stunted trees. This view soon gave way to one of attractive dwellings built of Yorkshire stone which lined both sides of the winding road as it began its descent towards the riverside village.

George Mason, while enjoying from his window seat a bird's-eye view of the long succession of front gardens, reviewed in his mind the few facts he already knew about the case in hand, while noting how popular rose cultivation was in these parts. 25 Foxwood Drive, Balderstones was the home of Mr. Leonard Parks, a special investigator for the Inland Revenue, based at their Manchester office. That he chose to dwell twelve miles to the north of that city did not surprise the detective at all. Judging by the homes that he was now admiring, this was a far more desirable milieu than any city center or inner suburb that he was aware of. It enjoyed fresh moorland air, low crime-rates and inviting country inns for convivial refreshment. The detective's main concern regarding Leonard Parks was that he had disappeared. His wife Justine had recently alerted the Yorkshire Constabulary of the fact. They, in turn, sensing wider implications beyond their normal purview, had enlisted the aid of Scotland Yard. Notified of his new assignment only the previous day, Mason had taken the midday train from London Euston, followed by the No.10 express bus from Manchester Piccadilly.

As his transport came to a halt at the terminus, the detective eased his large frame out of his seat and clambered down the rear stairs to alight in the quaintly-cobbled main square of Balderstones. A glance around him quickly took in its main features, fronted by a branch of Yorkshire Bank, an austere-looking Methodist church, a pub called The Red Lion and sundry small village shops, including a bakery and a newsagent's. He had barely walked ten paces when a squad car screeched to a halt beside him. Out sprang a young uniformed officer, who made his way nimbly round the far side of the vehicle to introduce himself.

"Constable Ron Higgins," he announced, extending his hand. "And you must be Inspector George Mason, from London?"

The detective nodded curtly, wincing slightly at the officer's firm grip.

"Sorry we could not arrange to pick you up in Manchester, Inspector," Higgins explained. "All police transports were tied up earlier at the youth sports day we hold every year at Wakefield, just across the Pennines."

"No problem," Mason replied. "I quite enjoyed the bus trip. It affords a grand view of the open moorland from the upper deck."

Constable Higgins, holding open the passenger door for the visitor to get in, seemed visibly relieved that the senior officer had not been inconvenienced. As the detective squeezed into the front seat, the vehicle reversed sharply before heading up a steep, tree-fringed road leading from the far corner of the square towards the open moors.

"When we get to Foxwood Drive," the younger man explained, "I shall just have time to introduce you to Justine Parks. I am on station duty from five o'clock, so I shall leave you in her good hands. Go easy on her; Inspector. She is beside herself with worry."

"I shall be as considerate as I can," George Mason assured him. "And do not concern yourself about me, if you have other commitments. After the interview, I shall make my way back down to the village on foot, book in at The Red Lion for the night and sample the dinner menu and the local brew."

Within a few minutes, the squad car suddenly took a sharp left turn before coming to a halt outside a three-story stone residence with mullioned windows.

"Originally a weaver's cottage," Higgins explained, noting Mason's interest in the unusual architecture as they approached the property through the garden gate. "It dates from the eighteenth century. The uppermost floor is where the weaver typically kept his loom."

"A cottage industry, in fact," George Mason knowledgeably observed, "which would have been in place long before the factory era."

"Exactly so," the constable said, with a broad smile. "We have quite a number of such dwellings here in Balderstones. They are much sought after. Very pricey, too."

"I can well imagine," Mason replied, as the oaken front door with a small window panel opened, to reveal a slim brunette clad in a print dress with a bold design he thought might be Marimekko, a Finnish style his wife Adele sometimes favored.

"Please step inside," the woman said, opening the door wider.

"Afraid I can't linger," Constable Higgins explained, consulting his watch. "I am already a little overdue back at the station. Justine, this is Inspector George Mason, from Scotland Yard. I am leaving you in his good hands."

"Thank you so much, Ron," she said as the young officer hurried back to his car. Addressing her visitor, she said: "Mind your head, Inspector. It is a low lintel."

The detective stooped instinctively and followed her into a spacious living-room with floral chair covers and matching curtains that offset the rather dark interior. The darkness was due to the narrow windows, he thought, designed to conserve heat during the Pennine winters.

"Please do take a seat, Inspector," Justine said, indicating one of two chairs placed by the window, with a small table set between them. "I was just about to brew a fresh pot of tea, if you would care to join me? I imagine you could use a pick-me-up after your long trip."

"That would suit me just fine, Mrs. Parks," the detective

replied, glad of the hospitality the area was noted for.

As she withdrew to the adjoining kitchen, Mason's eye took in the details of the room. It was paneled in dark wood, with well-stocked bookshelves, porcelain figurines on the mantelpiece and oil paintings of moorland scenes on the walls. He could well imagine winter evenings here, with a log fire blazing in the hearth and, since the cottage was situated on the upper rim of the village, the moorland gales and the driving rain. A glass of Burgundy and a good book completed his mental picture.

Justine soon returned, placing a laden tray on the occasional table and occupying the chair facing her visitor. She then did the honors, saying:

"Help yourself to milk and sugar," she said. "The biscuits are fresh from the village bakery."

George Mason did as bidden, adding milk but no sugar, while helping himself to two chocolate digestives.

"Now let us get straight to the point," his hostess said, in business-like fashion, after first sipping her tea.

"Your husband, I understand, has gone missing?" Mason said.

"I have not heard from him in two weeks," the young woman replied, with no attempt at concealing her concern.

"I gather he was away on business," the detective said. "Perhaps he has not had time to telephone?"

"That is not like Leonard at all," came the quick reply. "Always, when working away, he would call every couple of days, just to make sure I was all right. It can be quite lonely up here, especially at night." With a sweep of her arm, she indicated the broad swath of moorland beyond the living-room window.

George Mason, while tasting his tea, mentally framed a rather delicate question.

"Did your husband, in so far as you were aware," he asked, "have any significant problems? Money worries, for example, or difficulties with his job?"

Justine emphatically shook her head.

"We are quite comfortably off," she replied, glancing around the room appreciatively. "Leonard earns a good salary at the Inland Revenue in Manchester, while I teach part-time at the local school. Otherwise, we should not be living in an upscale property like this."

The detective glanced around the room admiringly as he partook of his refreshment, thinking this was as cozy an abode as one could wish for.

"His work environment was satisfactory then, Mrs. Parks?" he prompted, setting down his cup.

"Leonard was considered very professional at the Manchester office," Justine replied. "He worked very hard at it, putting in long hours. He was determined to be a success in his adopted country."

"You mean, he was not a native of England?"

"My husband came from Hungary, from near Budapest, as a matter of fact. He moved to England soon after our wedding, which was around the time Hungary joined the European Union.   That proved very convenient for us, since there is complete freedom of movement among member nations."

"You did not meet him in England, then?" the detective asked.

Justine again shook her head.

"We first met during a Danube River cruise," she said, with a wistful smile. "Leonard Farkas - for that was his surname before he anglicized it to Parks - was traveling with a group of Hungarian tourists. He introduced himself to the British party on the boat in order to practice his

English."

"And things developed from there?"

"He later visited England independently, and asked me to show him some of the sights. I readily obliged him, and that's how we really got to know each other. About two years later, after writing to each other, we got married."

"Would I be right in assuming, then, that there are no marital problems between you?" he enquired, as delicately as he could.

The young woman bridled slightly at the personal nature of the question, but gave no other reaction.

"You would be quite correct in your assumption," she replied, lowering her glance towards the service tray. "More tea, Inspector?"

The detective nudged his cup forward for a refill, while limiting himself to just one more biscuit ahead of what promised to be an ample pub dinner. How gracefully she poured, he noted, as if at one of the Queen's garden parties or at a ladies' gathering in the moorland village.

"What was your husband's background in Hungary?" he then asked.

"He was an investigator for an insurance company," Justine replied. "Magyar Life, I think its name was. His main duties involved investigating bogus claims and related matters."

"And what is the precise nature of his work at the Inland Revenue in the city of Manchester?"

"Something rather similar, in many ways," she informed him. "He investigates tax evasion."

"Then we have something in common," George Mason affably remarked, pleased that he had at last brought a smile to the woman's rather strained features.

"He made the transfer rather smoothly, from one job to

the other," his hostess explained. "It was really quite similar work, once he had learned the basics of Revenue procedures and had fully mastered the English language."

"I can appreciate that," Mason said admiringly, thinking it could hardly have been quite so easy as she was suggesting.

"Leonard speaks several languages," Justine said. "Which is why they ear-marked him for European assignments."

"Is that where your husband is now," he enquired, "on assignment in Europe?"

"I can give you his official itinerary," she replied.

Seeing that her visitor had drained his cup, she stood to return the tea-tray to the kitchen. When she reappeared, she switched on the computer on the far side of the room and beckoned George Mason to join her.

"I have been assisting Leonard with routine clerical work," she explained, accessing one of the desktop files. "If you have a notebook handy, you could jot down the names and addresses relevant to his current schedule."

George Mason scanned the computer screen closely. Ignoring the financial details, since he was not concerned with tax evasion, he wrote down the names, occupations and last-known addresses of three individuals, all of whom had run afoul of the British tax authorities in recent months.

"Quite a spread, geographically," he remarked as Justine closed the Internet file as soon as he had made some notes. She then switched off the computer and returned to her seat by the window.

"All the way from Ostend to Budapest," she said, with a heavy sigh.

"Overland, too," the detective remarked. "That involves quite a bit of rail travel."

"Leonard just loves the European rail network," she explained.

"Very speedy and comfortable, especially in the dining-cars," Mason agreed. "I have used them myself, from time to time. I much prefer it to traveling by air."

"It seemed the easiest way to do things," she added, "covering the entire route in convenient stages. The last leg of his journey was in fact to be undertaken by boat, from Vienna to Budapest, along the River Danube. He promised to take photographs to remind us both of our first meeting."

"He may simply have encountered some small difficulty along the way," Mason said, in an attempt to be reassuring. "But he has not, in so far as I am aware, contacted any of our European embassies. At least, he had not done so before I left London. Otherwise, they would have informed the Yorkshire police, who would not then have needed to enlist the help of Scotland Yard."

"Leonard would be loath to do something like that," Justine remarked, "except out of dire necessity. He is a very self-reliant person."

"Then I expect he can very well look after himself," Mason observed. "In some sense, his final destination would be something of a homecoming."

"When he reached Budapest, he was going to stay with an old college friend called Milos," Justine explained. "They have not been able to meet up again, for one reason and another, in the past several years."

George Mason then wondered if Leonard Parks, having completed his tax enquiries in good order, had not been carousing his way down the Danube, catching up with old college chums. He might simply have been too occupied to ring his wife.

"What would also be helpful," he remarked, "is a list of

hotels where your husband planned to stay."

"You can obtain that from his Manchester office," Justine replied. "His secretary made the reservations on his behalf, some weeks ago."

"I shall call at the Inland Revenue premises first thing tomorrow morning," the detective said, "on my way to the railway station. It is just possible that by then the staff may have received news of him."

"I sincerely hope so," Justine said, with feeling.

She then gave her visitor a rather concerned look.

"Afraid I cannot offer you dinner, Inspector," she added. "It is ladies' bridge evening at The Cross Keys Inn. I tried to excuse myself in the current circumstances, but they are counting on me to make up the numbers."

"Then by all means go," Mason urged, rising to his feet. "It will help take your mind off things. And do not concern yourself about me. I am an old hand at this sort of thing, and I quite enjoy country inns. I will check in at the Red Lion down in the village, have a leisurely dinner and catch up with the business and sports news in *The Times*."

"They do an excellent Yorkshire pudding there," a more buoyant Justine suggested. "You might like to try it with the roast beef."

"I shall certainly give it serious consideration," he replied, moving towards the door. "Oh, and by the way, I noticed the letters FMP at the head of your husband's computer file. Do you happen to know what they stand for?"

The young woman, evidently at a loss for an explanation, shook her head.

"Leonard heads all his files that way," she said. "He also has them printed on his office stationery, curiously enough. I did once ask him the reason, but he was evasive. I did not press him in case he thought I was prying."

"Something of personal significance, I expect," Mason suggested, with the curious impression that he had seen an identical monogram somewhere before, yet he could not quite recall where.

"You *will* let me know, Inspector," she called after him, as he exited and headed up the path to the garden gate, "as soon as you hear anything?"

"I most certainly shall," he promised, with a wave of his hand, as he turned into Foxwood Drive for the walk back down to the village, increasing his gait as he spotted storm clouds gathering over the Pennines.

*

Manchester was in a mid-morning bustle by the time George Mason reached it by express bus from Balderstones the following day. He alighted at Piccadilly Gardens, that oasis in the city center often frequented by office workers eating snack lunches, and by the occasional resident walking his dog. He had visited the city several times previously, finding its lay-out to his liking, with its broad thoroughfares and commercial buildings of fairly uniform design, most of them dating from the Victorian era. Traversing the gardens, where late-season flowers were in bloom, he made his way down Market Street, a pedestrian precinct fronted by department stores and small retail outlets, mingling with the crowd of shoppers hunting bargains in the sales. A left turn just past the newly-installed tramway took him by the imposing Royal Exchange, where cotton futures were once traded, and on into Albert Square with its imposing neo-Gothic town hall. A side-street off the square brought him to Cavendish

Street, where he soon located the offices of Inland Revenue.

Feeling a sense of relief that his own tax affairs were in good order, he took the lift to the third floor and passed through a door marked Special Services. A receptionist took his name and invited him to take a seat. Moments later, a young woman who vaguely reminded him of Justine Parks - she was of the same build, with similar chin-length dark hair - entered the room and led him through to a rear office.

"We are extremely concerned about Mr. Parks," the woman began. "Not a word from him since he left England. His wife must be beside herself with worry."

"She is bearing up," the detective said. "I just got back from Balderstones. I had a long chat with Justine last evening. She told me, among other things, that I could get a list of her husband's hotel bookings from you. You will be his secretary, I take it?"

"Charlene Jones," the young woman said, introducing herself. "And yes, I have been Mr. Parks' personal assistant for the past eighteen months."

"George Mason, from Scotland Yard," he announced.

"I am glad to see that the police are taking this matter seriously," Miss Jones remarked, with a look of approval.

"It does not come any more serious than Special Branch," her visitor replied. "In any case, Continental Europe is not really the province of a regional police force such as Yorkshire. They have enough on their hands, what with drug-pedaling, burglaries, traffic violations and similar routine crimes."

"You can say that again," the secretary replied, clicking on her computer to print off a short list of hotels, which she passed to the detective.

Mason perused it carefully.

"L'Ocean, Ostend," he read aloud. "That would be his first port of call?"

Charlene Jones nodded in agreement.

"The well-known sommelier, Colin Sutton, was the first person Mr. Parks intended to interview," she said.

"Sommelier?" Mason queried, not quite sure what the word meant.

"The wine expert," the young woman informed him. "The person in charge of the cellars at a hotel or upscale restaurant. He may also recommend which wines to serve with which dishes."

"I get it," the detective replied, committing the unfamiliar term to memory while examining the list of names Justine Parks had given him, to match them up with the hotel bookings.

"One thing puzzles me," he remarked, after a while. "Perhaps you can enlighten me?"

"I shall do my level best," the secretary assured him.

"All these names seem to be of persons living and working in Europe. How is it then, that they have fallen foul of the Inland Revenue?"

"A good question," Charlene Jones said, with an indulgent smile at her visitor's innocence in tax matters. "Mr. Sutton, for example, works the summer season on the Belgian coast, namely at Ostend. During the remainder of the year, he is employed at a leading London hotel, where his earnings are liable to UK income tax. It is his gratuities, or tips if you prefer, over the past few years that mainly interest us."

"You mean that he has come clean about his salary, but has not disclosed his tips?" George Mason asked.

Charlene Jones nodded.

"In the sort of milieu in which Colin Sutton operates, tips could amount to a substantial sum. Since they are not recorded on pay-slips, we rely on people employed in the hospitality industry to come up with a realistic figure. Earnings made abroad, on the other hand, are only taxed here if the money is brought into Britain."

"You have a ballpark figure in mind, based on the nature and locale of the work?"

"Precisely, Inspector," Charlene replied.

"And these other names?" the detective then enquired.

"Although they mainly live abroad, they have sufficient financial affairs in this country to be of interest to the Inland Revenue. Professor Paul Jarvis, for example, runs courses here during the early part of the summer, for the Open University."

"All very complex," Mason said. "But I expect you have everything at your finger-tips?"

"We endeavor to do so," came the quick reply. "Our Mr. Parks has been very efficient at recovering monies owed to the Treasury. A dedicated public servant, if ever I met one."

"I can appreciate that," her visitor said.

"There is something else that you should be aware of," the young woman then said, "before you embark on your own investigations. You *are* going to investigate, aren't you, Inspector?"

"Why, of course I am," George Mason assured her. "That is the whole point of my presence here today."

"What I really meant to ask," she hastily added, slightly flustered, "is whether your investigation is imminent, not something you are going to put on a back burner."

"Leonard Parks is top priority in London," the detective emphasized. "The Home Office is breathing down our necks. Any day now, questions will be raised in the House of Commons about a missing public servant. Now tell me what else I should know."

"The day before Leonard Parks left this office," Charlene Jones informed him, "we had a tip-off from an anonymous source. Leonard thought it might be just a hoax, but he was determined to look into it in any event. It came from someone who claimed to be an employee of a private Swiss bank. He gave the names of dozens of British nationals for whom his bank had been arranging off-shore accounts in the Cayman Islands in recent years."

"To evade tax in the United Kingdom?" Mason asked, immediately getting the picture.

"Precisely, Inspector. And there could be some very large sums of money involved."

"So how does this concern my brief?" the detective wanted to know.

"Two of those names," she replied, with a triumphant look, "are also on your list of people to interview!"

"Tell me more!" he urged, preparing to note them down.

The secretary flicked her attractive fringe to one side and briefly consulted her files.

"First, we have Dieter Lutz, an antiquarian living at Zurich," she said. "There is also the Paul Jarvis I already mentioned, who is Visiting Professor of English at the University of Zell, in the Austrian Tyrol. Professor Jarvis has several sources of income, apart from his work for the Open University, which are of interest to the Inland Revenue. One of them is the royalties he receives from his widely-used textbooks. We suspect that those monies may well have found their way off-shore."

George Mason, thinking there was not a whole lot he could do about that, thanked the young woman for her information and made his way back down to street-level. Once outdoors, he strolled back across the cobbled Albert Square in the direction of Tommy's Chop House, noted for such local dishes as Lancashire hot pot and shepherd's pie. It would be crowded at this hour with workers from nearby offices, but worth a visit nonetheless. The next London train, from Manchester Piccadilly, did not leave until 2.05 p.m., allowing him plenty of time. Since it was an afternoon train, he foresaw no difficulty in obtaining a seat.

CHAPTER TWO

When George Mason entered the second-floor suite of offices at Scotland Yard the following morning at just turned 9.00 a.m., to report his findings, his immediate superior, Chief Inspector Bill Harrington, was waiting for him. To Mason's not altogether agreeable surprise, the head of the C.I.D., Superintendent James Maitland, was also present.

"Had a useful trip up north?" Harrington genially enquired, inviting George Mason to take a seat.

"I think I now have sufficient information to make a useful start," Mason cautiously replied, wondering why the superintendent, who was normally briefed in private by Harrington, had chosen to sit in on the meeting.

"You only *think* you have?" Harrington challenged. "Come now, Inspector Mason, don't be coy. The Superintendent here is taking a special interest in this case." He glanced in the direction of Maitland, who was standing by the window, observing the hub-bub in the street below.

On hearing his name mentioned, James Maitland turned his attention directly to the new arrival.

"I gather," he began, cordially enough, "that you have just been to the Pennine village of Balderstones to interview Leonard Parks' wife?"

"That is correct, sir."

"And how did you find her?"

"Very concerned that she has not heard from her husband in two weeks," Mason replied.

"That is only to be expected, in the circumstances," the superintendent said. "Apart from that, is her personal situation satisfactory?"

George Mason felt puzzled at this show of concern for the wife of a missing income tax official. Wasn't this, after all, just another routine missing persons enquiry?

"She appears to be quite comfortably off, and bearing up well," he replied. "She occupies an old weaver's cottage, one of the prime residences in Balderstones, situated on the edge of the moors. She takes an active a part in village life."

James Maitland nodded approvingly.

"I am pleased to hear that," he remarked. "Now listen carefully Mason, since I can only spare a few minutes. The Home Office is taking a strong interest in this case. They are very concerned that an Inland Revenue officer has gone missing in the line of duty and are anticipating questions being raised in the House of Commons. We are relying on you, with your experience in European assignments, to get to the bottom of this business as quickly as possible. You are to leave for the Continent without delay."

"I understand perfectly, sir," George Mason dutifully replied.

"Oh, and one more thing, Inspector," the superintendent added. "I am arranging for Detective Sergeant Alison Aubrey, formerly of the Sussex C.I.D., to assist you again, in view of the good reports you gave of her on previous assignments."

Mason returned a broad smile.

"I appreciate that, Superintendent," Mason replied.

"I have full confidence in you both," Maitland then said. "You shall have a fairly generous expense allowance. An operation like this cannot be done on a shoe-string. I want it done expeditiously, with results, to get the Home Secretary off my back."

After the senior official left, Bill Harrington turned to his colleague.

"There you have it, Inspector, in a nutshell," he said, with a bland smile. "If James Maitland wants quick results, you had better get cracking. How soon could you leave, realistically?"

"In a couple of days, perhaps," Mason replied. "There will be a few things to sort out on the home front beforehand."

"Excellent," the other said. "I knew we could count on you. Take the next couple of days off for personal arrangements. We shall book you a place on the cross-Channel ferry from Dover. Collect a wad of signed checks from the accounts department and fill in the amounts you need as you go. Any good European bank will cash them for you. And do not take Maitland's remarks about expenses too liberally. We all have to work within our budget, which has just been cut back in the national economy drive."

"And Sergeant Aubrey?" George Mason enquired, rising to his feet.

"She will be tied up for the next few days on a training course. I shall arrange for her to fly out to Zurich to catch up with you there. I shall give you her flight details before you leave, so that you can meet her at Kloten Airport."

*

Three days later, George Mason was comfortably ensconced in a window seat of the boat train from Victoria Station as it sped through the Kent countryside, hop-growing country mainly, dotted with oast-houses, on his way to the Channel port of Dover. His wife Adele had driven him to the station, before heading out to Berkshire to spend a few days with an old school friend, who often invited her to stay during her husband's absences. Admonishing him to take good care of himself and keep in regular touch by telephone, she had hugged him good-bye and disappeared into the crowd of commuters arriving off suburban trains. Mason ordered coffee from the passing trolley and opened up his copy of *The Times,* mainly to check the cricket scores, including the Third Test Match between England and New Zealand. Thus absorbed, the time passed quickly. In another two hours he was standing on the foredeck of a car-ferry named the *Dieppe,* as it eased its way slowly out of the sheltered harbor and into the open waters of the English Channel, one of the busiest sea-lanes in the world.

Following a choppy crossing, which he had spent strolling the decks to stretch his legs and get the benefit of the sea air while watching the chalk cliffs recede into distance, he disembarked clutching his valise at the Ostend terminal. From there, he proceeded along the broad promenade protected by a strong sea-wall, noting the number and variety of restaurants, mainly for seafood, while wondering how, in this not typically tourist city, they all managed to attract custom. But wasn't food-and-drink the Belgians' great passion in life? And on this fine summer evening there seemed to be plenty of visitors about, family groups returning from the beach and yachtsmen securing their craft in the busy marina after a day on the open sea. There were English voices, too, to be heard now and then among the predominantly French and Flemish. Very occasionally, he caught a pronounced American accent he thought might be from the Midwest. Just beyond the yachting marina, a bustling fish market was in progress, with fishwives calling out an amazing variety of wares and tourists buying snacks, in addition to discriminating buyers stocking up for the restaurant trade. It was, in fact, the sort of ambience that appealed strongly to George Mason. He resolved, once he had checked into his hotel, to follow the broad sweep of the promenade round the headland and find himself a small eatery where he could fill out his evening over an enjoyable meal, with perhaps a glass or two of chilled Muscadet to accompany it.

He soon located L'Ocean Hotel, in a prominent position about a hundred yards from the ferry terminal. To judge from its size, it was one of the premier establishments in the port city. He mounted the short flight of steps leading to the main entrance, crossed the busy foyer and approached Reception, where he checked in and received the key to a room on the top floor. On entering it and crossing to the window, he was pleased to note that he had a good view out to sea, spotting the *Dieppe* as it was easing out of the harbor on its return trip to Dover. Unpacking his few belongings, he tested the bed for firmness, had a quick shower and took the lift back down to the foyer. The desk clerk seemed a little apprehensive at the visitor's sudden reappearance, as if expecting some formal complaint.

"Everything is to your satisfaction, Monsieur Mason?" he cautiously enquired.

"Quite satisfactory," the detective replied. "It is a nice room, especially for the ocean view."

"In what way can I be of assistance?"

"I am trying to trace a fellow countryman," the detective said. "A Mr. Leonard Parks, who I believe stayed at this hotel about two weeks ago."

The clerk, happy to oblige, consulted his computerized records.

"I remember him well," he explained, after a short while. "Mr. Parks arrived here on August 21 and checked out two days later. Our sommelier, Mr. Sutton, gave him a lift to the train station, as I recall."

"Would it be possible to speak with Mr. Sutton?"

"That would be rather difficult just now," the other said. "Mr. Sutton is on duty in the main restaurant all evening. But I can book you an appointment first thing tomorrow morning, if you so wish. Are you in the wine business, Monsieur Mason?"

"Er...no," the visitor haltingly replied. "It is more in the nature of a personal matter."

"Ten o'clock?"

"That would suit me fine."

"Mr. Sutton's office is at the far end of the corridor to the right," the clerk explained, with a wave of his arm in the general direction, before answering a phone-call. "I shall tell him to expect you then."

George Mason thanked him and left the hotel, determined to make the most of a free evening at the coast. Continuing along the promenade away from the ferry terminal, he soon discovered a broad expanse of sandy beach, where family groups lingered in the evening sunshine, sharing space with seagulls and oyster catchers seeking pickings from the ebbing tide. This stretch of seafront was also the main locus of outdoor restaurants, now beginning to fill with early diners. In an hour or so, when he had worked up a good appetite, he would visit one, order a light dinner and fill out the remaining daylight hours with a half-carafe of wine and a Dutch cigar, watching the yachts with brightly-colored sails as they tacked across the bay. It figured, he told himself, that the sommelier would be tied up all evening at such a high-class hotel; but at least he had ascertained that Leonard Parks had met with Colin Sutton, according to plan.

*

Colin Sutton eyed his visitor quizzically as he ushered him the following morning into his cramped office at the far end of a corridor leading off the hotel foyer. He was a rotund man of short stature, with a ruddy complexion and thinning strands of blond hair, dressed in a light-tan jacket and plum-colored bow tie.

"You are not in the trade, are you, Mr….?" he said, rather testily.

"*Inspector* Mason," the detective emphasized, producing official ID, "from Scotland Yard."

The sommelier's eyes widened and his fleshy features clouded perceptibly.

"Please take a seat, Inspector," he said, more deferentially, clearing away some of the desk clutter in the shape of promotional materials, trade samples, cigar wrappers and suchlike. "To what do I owe the honor of a visit from the Metropolitan Police?"

George Mason eased himself into the vacant chair and quickly surveyed the small room, complete with a bookcase holding what appeared to be wine atlases, gastronomy tomes, travel guides and a framed portrait of what he took to be the wine expert's two children.

"I understand, Mr. Sutton," he began, "that you recently had an interview with a Mr. Leonard Parks, of the Inland Revenue."

The sommelier frowned perceptibly, evidently wondering how the C.I.D. had got wind of his tax affairs.

"That is correct," he replied. "We had a frank discussion right here in this office. He sat where you are sitting now."

"About monies owed to the British Treasury?"

Colin Sutton noisily cleared his throat and gave a curt nod of agreement.

"I am not under arrest, am I, Inspector?" he asked, apprehensively.

George Mason returned an ironic smile.

"Let me make it clear from the outset, Mr. Sutton," he said, "that I am not here on behalf of the Inland Revenue per se."

The sommelier gave a sigh of relief.

"Then what brings you to Ostend, Inspector?" he asked, in some puzzlement.

"Mr. Parks interviewed you, I believe, regarding tax evasion in the United Kingdom, where I understand you are employed during the winter months. Can you expand on that?"

Colin Sutton shifted uncomfortably in his chair, averting his eyes from the detective's penetrating gaze.

"I had a long discussion with him," he said, gazing at the wall calendar, "mainly about gratuities I received over a period of years during my tenure at the Serpentine Hotel in Mayfair."

"You must have earned quite a large amount in tips to spark the interest of the tax authorities," Mason remarked, "since they allow a certain latitude in that area to catering personnel, who sometimes exist on relatively low pay."

The sommelier smiled ruefully.

"The Serpentine is one of the West End's leading hotels," he said. "It has many wealthy visitors, particularly from the Middle East. I must admit that I have made a fair amount of money there over the years. Almost as much as my regular salary in fact."

"Because they valued your expertise?"

"Exactly, Inspector," came the prompt reply. "They needed, above all, to impress their guests and business associates. Gratuities tend to flow quite freely in such circumstances."

George Mason carefully weighed his remarks, glancing appreciatively around him at all the paraphernalia of the wine trade.

"You have a very lucrative profession," he observed, with a touch almost of envy.

Colin Sutton returned a rather self-satisfied smile.

"I shall gladly give you a brief tour of our cellars, if that would interest you," he said, hoping to impress his unexpected visitor. "They are by far the best-stocked in this port city."

"I should like that very much," the detective replied, thinking that he might pick up some useful tips. "But first, tell me the result of your interview with Leonard Parks."

"I produced a rough estimate of my gratuities over the last three years. He could not legally go back beyond that and, after some haggling, we finally arrived at a figure he thought realistic and acceptable. He then informed me that I would be receiving a revised tax assessment for each of the last three years, and that I was to pay the amounts due, plus interest, promptly. Or face prosecution."

"So it all ended amicably, on a positive note?" Mason queried.

"Very much so," the sommelier agreed. "I invited him to lunch in the hotel restaurant, uncorking one of our best vintages for the occasion - a 1973 Crozes Hermitage."

"I imagine he appreciated that," his visitor said, approvingly. "So what happened next, after the gourmet lunch?"

"I drove him directly to the train station."

"Do you happen to know what his destination was?"

"I seem to recall he was on his way to Switzerland," Sutton replied. "Zurich, I think he said."

"Did you actually see him board the train?"

"I was on my way to a conference at Ghent," the other explained. "And I was a bit pushed for time after the leisurely lunch. I just dropped him off at the station forecourt, so I can only assume that he boarded his train."

"Thank you very much, Mr. Sutton," George Mason remarked, in conclusion. "You have been very helpful. Now, how about that wine tour?"

The sommelier sprang to his feet and happily led the way down a flight of stone steps to the cellars, where he quickly introduced the detective to his favorite wine-growing regions. Austria, to his visitor's surprise, featured prominently.

"We have just begun stocking a selection of English wines," Colin Sutton explained, "for the more adventurous palate."

"I read that viticulture is taking off big-time in England," Mason said.

"There are now hundreds of vineyards in Britain," the expert rejoined. "It is one interesting result of global warming. Areas of northern Europe that were not formerly conducive to viticulture are now coming into their own."

"You amaze me, Mr. Sutton," the detective responded,

as his guide offered him a complimentary glass of a white wine bottled on the Isle of Wight.

CHAPTER THREE

On taking leave of the bon-vivant sommelier, who seemed to be resolving his issues with the British tax authorities, George Mason called at police headquarters to ascertain if they had any knowledge of a British citizen named Leonard Parks. Nothing came up in their computer records and he was informed that there had been no murders, kidnappings or missing person events so far this year in the port city. There had been several muggings, mainly of tourists. The duty officer then, as a matter of routine, placed a call to the local morgue, which also drew a blank. The detective was thankful for that. On his way afterwards by taxi to catch the Zurich train, he felt reasonably confident that Leonard Parks had left Ostend in one piece and had taken an inter-city train south, to reach Switzerland.

It was a fascinating trip, through the cities of Cologne, with its imposing cathedral, Dusseldorf, Mainz and Freiburg, viewed mainly from the comfortable dining-car, where he took an extended lunch, while observing the heavily-laden barges navigating the Rhein. It was late evening when he reached Zurich, covering on foot the short distance between the near-deserted Hauptbahnhof and Hotel Adler, noting how quiet the city was at this hour, with just a few pedestrians strolling down the Limmatquai, the main artery running alongside the river from the point where it left the lake. The walk, he felt, would do him good after sitting many hours in the train, in company with relaxed travelers accustomed to long Continental rail journeys. Having already had a substantial meal, he decided to spend the last hour of the day in his well-appointed hotel room, serving himself a whisky-and-soda from the mini-bar, while gleaning what he could from the television news, delivered in German.

Breakfast the next day was served in a ground-floor restaurant with typical alpine motifs. It overlooked the River Limmat, where he espied from his place in the buffet queue the moored launches being readied for the tourist trade, also catching through part-open windows the raucous cries of the gulls circling overhead. The fare was simple enough, but satisfying, consisting of cereals with yogurt, cold cuts, a selection of Swiss cheeses and fresh coffee. Having skipped dinner the previous evening, he found he had a good appetite, helping himself to a portion of each item and repairing to a table in the far corner of the room, well away from the cramped serving area, so that he could gather his thoughts for the day ahead. Already, on arrival, he had ascertained from the hotel clerk that the tax investigator, Leonard Parks, had booked into the Adler on August 23, and that he had settled his account and departed two days later. So far, so good.

His main concern that day was to locate and interview the second name on his short list of tax-evaders. Dieter Lutz, because his name was so un-British, did not sound to the detective the sort of person likely to fall foul of the British tax authorities. But who was he, George Mason, to question information provided by the Inland Revenue, in the person of Miss Charlene Jones? And why was the

Home Office so concerned about the progress of this case and the probability of questions in the House of Commons? Why, also, had Superintendent Maitland seen fit to detail Alison Aubrey to accompany him, when the young sergeant had recently been assigned her own caseload, after gaining valuable experience assisting him on previous enquiries? The uneasy thought entered his mind, as he crossed the floor of the restaurant for a refill of coffee, that her real role might be to check up on him in some way. He had had problems in the past with the superintendent over the way he handled some aspects of his job, particularly those involving European travel. But Maitland's concerns had normally been channeled through Bill Harrington. Only six months ago, in fact, the chief inspector had tackled him about a spa bill in Stockholm, where Mason had merely used the sauna.

As he was on the point of leaving the restaurant, a hotel employee quickly approached him.

"The manager, Herr Staheli," the young woman said, handing him a small package, "asked me to give you this."

George Mason opened the sealed envelope and found that it contained, to his considerable surprise, a leather-bound pocket diary.

"We came across it in a drawer of Mr. Parks' bedroom the day after he checked out," the woman explained. "Herr Staheli thought that, since you have been enquiring about Mr. Parks, you may be able to meet up with him in the near future and return it to him."

"How curious," Mason commented, placing the object in his jacket pocket to peruse later, thinking it might contain some useful leads.

"Then I shall inform the manager that you have accepted responsibility for it," the young woman said, with evident relief.

"Tell Herr Staheli that I can offer no assurances," the detective said, "but I shall do my best."

"That is very helpful of you, Herr Mason," the employee replied. "I shall inform the manager at once."

George Mason walked with her as far as the hotel foyer, so that she could give him directions to Schipfe. It turned out to be situated on the opposite bank of the river, not a great distance from Hotel Adler. A clear sky greeted him as he made his way across the stone bridge, glancing at the tourist launch passing beneath it, some of whose passengers waved gaily up at him. He eventually reached a covered walk running for some distance alongside the river. The boutiques he passed were mainly dedicated to various crafts, including silverware, jewelry, wood carvings, glassware, vintage maps and model yachts. He paused for a moment to admire a scale replica of the famous tea clipper, the *Cutty Sark*, before espying the name Dieter Lutz, in Gothic script, above the window of an antiquarian bookstore, next to a shop displaying Russian icons.

A thin, elderly gentleman, with wispy white hair and wire-rimmed spectacles, who was engaged in re-binding an atlas, put aside his task and greeted the detective as he entered.

"Nice premises you have here," the visitor remarked, appreciatively. "The whole arcade, in fact, is quite fascinating."

"Isn't it so?" the owner replied, in a heavy accent. "Schipfe stands at the outer edge of what was formerly a walled city named Turicum. The fortifications in olden times came right down here to the riverside, making attack with siege towers and similar military contraptions virtually impossible."

"The Romans were experts at defense," Mason readily agreed. "Take Hadrian's Wall, for example, extending clear across the north of England, from one coast to the other."

"I have seen it for myself," Dieter Lutz replied. "Even hiked most of its length, at one time or another. But you did not come here to discuss Classical Rome, Herr...?"

"Mason," his visitor replied. "Inspector George Mason, to be precise, of Scotland Yard."

The bookseller's genial smile faded, as he peered quizzically into the other's eyes, wondering if he should take this surprise announcement at face value.

"Do you wish to see my ID?" the detective asked, noting his hesitation.

. The bookseller brushed the suggestion aside.

"If you said you were the Crown Prince, I would believe you," he replied, with conviction. "You have a genuine look about you, a quality one does not so often encounter these days. Now tell me, what exactly is it that you require at Buchhandlung Lutz?"

"I think you may already suspect the reason for my visit."

Dieter Lutz retreated into the well of his shop, leaning back against his book-binding bench, as if for support.

"It is about income tax, isn't it?" he said, deciding that the game was up. "You have come to arrest me!"

His visitor gave a broad smile and slowly shook his head.

"I am much more concerned about the Inland Revenue official who I believe may have interviewed you about two weeks ago," he said.

"You are not here on behalf of the tax authorities then?" the other asked, visibly relieved.

"The Inland Revenue know all about your financial

affairs," Mason said. "They are even aware of your off-shore accounts in the Cayman Islands, arranged through a Swiss bank."

The bookseller returned an ironic smile.

"Inspector Mason," he slyly remarked, "you know as well as I do that tax avoidance, as opposed to tax evasion, is not a crime in Switzerland. On the contrary, it is positively encouraged. In some quarters, it is even considered a civic duty. I said as much to Mr. Leonard Parks, but he had difficulty accepting the notion."

George Mason laughed out loud, at what he took to be mild hyperbole on the other's part. Dieter Lutz evidently had a keen sense of humor, but beneath it he was making a valid point.

"All the same," he said, "it would interest me to know in what circumstances you fell foul of the British tax authorities. And how, with your German surname, you come to speak English so fluently."

"Both matters are quite easily explained," the antiquarian replied. "For many years, I owned a bookshop in Bloomsbury, a stone's throw from the University of London, in order to exploit the student textbook trade. I was even a special consultant at the university for a while, in medieval manuscripts. For the History Department, under Professor Archibald Todd."

"Please tell me more," an intrigued George Mason urged.

"My mother was English," Lutz explained. "She first met my father in the later stages of World War 11, while serving in the Royal Army Nursing Corps behind the front lines in the push through the Ardennes. My father, Volker Lutz, was wounded in the course of a panzer offensive and taken prisoner. Mother nursed him back to health."

"Amazing," Mason observed, "how romance can spring

out of so much carnage and devastation. It renews one's faith in human nature."

"It was a love-match all right," the other said. "And I am the younger of two sons. Mother encouraged me to set up shop in London, where she had raised us. Some years after the war, my parents moved to Zurich, where my father had obtained a lectureship at the Institute of Technology."

"So you decided at some point to transfer your business here, because of a family connection?" the detective asked.

"My parents died years ago," came the reply. "They owned a small villa by the lake, which was passed on to my brother and me as joint owners. My brother Rainer lives at Frankfurt and is content for me to occupy it. Two years ago, a sharp increase in property taxes cut into my London profits. I was also losing business to on-line retailers, so I decided to transfer my stock to Zurich, sell the Bloomsbury premises and invest the proceeds."

"Which explains the Inland Revenue's interest in you?" Mason prompted.

"Capital gains tax," Lutz ruefully replied, "on the realized value of my Bloomsbury shop."

"A considerable sum of money, I imagine," the detective remarked, "considering how property values, especially in central London, have increased in recent years. Hence Mr. Parks' interest in you?"

"He tried to persuade me to do the decent thing," the other said. "After all, he was only doing his job. I did, in fact, offer him a nominal sum, to placate him. He eventually agreed, after a lot of haggling, to refer the matter back to his office in Manchester."

"So the meeting ended on a cordial note?" Mason enquired.

"Parks was far from satisfied, to tell you the truth. But he really had no option, since I am now a Swiss citizen. I renounced British citizenship precisely to avoid British taxes, which are far more onerous than the Swiss."

The detective thought that sounded like a reasonable explanation.

"Did you notice anything unusual about Leonard Parks' manner at the time?" he asked. "Did he, for example, seem unduly preoccupied? Perhaps worried about something?"

The bookseller tugged lightly on his wispy beard as he considered the matter.

"He did seem a bit concerned about travel arrangements to Zell, in the Austrian Tyrol," he replied. "So I consulted my European Rail handbook and worked out a route for him, through Innsbruck. Apart from that, he seemed like a normal income tax official to me...if you could describe anyone in that calling as normal."

George Mason returned an ironic smile. The same remark might apply, he mused, to any public official, including himself. He fished inside his jacket pocket and drew out Parks' diary. Dieter Lutz, surrounded every day as he was with old books, struck him as the sort of individual whose knowledge would cover the most arcane subjects.

"Tell me," he said, showing him the front page of the diary, where the monogram was prominently inscribed, "do the letters F.M.P. mean anything to you?"

Dieter Lutz took the diary and studied the monogram for a few moments, knitting his brows in puzzlement. At that point, a customer entered the shop, commanding his attention.

"Leave it with me, Inspector Mason," he said. "I shall see if I can come up with something when we close for lunch. Could you possibly call back later today?"

"That would suit me fine," Mason said, checking his watch. "I have to go over to Kloten Airport just now, in any case, to meet a young colleague of mine off a flight from Heathrow."

With that, he left the antiquarian to deal with his customer and walked briskly through a maze of narrow, cobbled alleys in the Altstadt, the well-preserved medieval part of the city, until he reached Bahnhofstrasse. After cashing one of his expense checks at Union Bank, he proceeded to the main station, crossed the busy concourse and waited for the next shuttle service to Kloten.

*

Detective Sergeant Alison Aubrey caught an initial glimpse of the Swiss countryside as the British Airways jetliner began its descent towards the runway. Her eager eye took in the undulating landscape and the snaking course of a large river she took to be the upper Rhine, which she had first seen at Basel on a previous assignment with Inspector Mason. She was now looking forward to renewing her acquaintance with Zurich.

George Mason was waiting to greet her as she came through Customs.

"Bang on time, Sergeant," he remarked, affably. "Had a good trip?"

"A very smooth flight, thankfully," Alison said. "Just under two hours from Heathrow."

"Glad to have you back on board," he said. "It has been a while."

"It was something of a surprise to me, George, when Superintendent Maitland asked me to team up with you for this investigation."

"Because you have been handling your own caseload recently?"

The young sergeant nodded.

"Maitland seems to attach particular importance to solving this business," Mason then said. "The Home Office is breathing down his neck. He may consider that two heads are better than one, especially in view of the good reports I gave of your performance on previous assignments."

"That was big of you, George," his colleague said. "I am grateful for it. It has helped my career prospects quite a lot."

"Do not mention it, Alison," Mason generously allowed. "Incidentally, are you at all hungry?"

Alison smilingly shook her head, pleased at his concern.

"Not immediately," she replied. "I had a light meal on the plane, which should last me until dinner."

"Let me handle that," he said, stooping to grasp her bulky valise.

"It is rather heavy," Alison cautioned.

George Mason, ignoring her remark, hefted it onto a coin-operated cart, which he nimbly steered down the long sloping ramp to the train platform. .

"First thing is to get you checked into the hotel," he said, as they settled into their seats waiting for the shuttle service to depart, which it duly did within minutes. "Take what time you need to unpack and freshen up. Since this will be only your second visit to Zurich, take a stroll round the city center to re-orientate yourself, while I take care of a little outstanding business. We could meet up again at six o'clock for an early dinner and a briefing. How does that sound?"

Alison Aubrey smiled in agreement.

"I am really happy, George," she said, "to team up with you again, especially on another foreign assignment. More useful experience for me."

"I do not doubt that, Alison," the detective replied. "All in all, we may do a fair amount of traveling."

"I am keenly looking forward to it," she replied.

For the remainder of the twenty-minute journey, he lapsed into silence and admired the scenery, as his companion flicked through the copy of *Cosmopolitan* she had bought at Heathrow.

On arrival at the Hauptbahnhof, he grasped her luggage and led the way across the bridge over the River Limmat to Hotel Adler, a short walk along the Limmatquai, and waited until she had checked in and taken the lift up to her room before heading straight back to Dieter Lutz's bookshop at Schipfe. It was just turned one o'clock by the time he reached it, half-way through the proprietor's lunch-hour. He had to knock on the shuttered front entrance to gain admittance. The proprietor, munching on a salami roll, greeted him cordially.

"Please step inside, Inspector Mason," he said, laying his half-eaten snack aside and bolting the door behind them. "We may be in luck. F.M.P., I discovered from one of my classical sources, may possibly represent the Latin motto *Faciant meliora potentes,* attributed to Pliny. Pliny the Elder, to be precise."

"You have me there," the detective confessed. "Latin was never my strong suit."

"A rough English translation might be 'Let those who can do better'."

"Whoever *those* are."

"I think I can help you there, Inspector," the antiquarian said, with a twinkle in his eye. "Only very few individuals would know this, since it is a closely-guarded secret, but the same motto has been adopted in recent years by the Potenti."

"And who might they be?" an intrigued George Mason enquired.

"The top echelon of the Illuminati."

"I am still none the wiser, Herr Lutz," his perplexed visitor confessed.

"The Illuminati are a secret society said to have been founded in Bavaria in the eighteenth century," the other explained. "They are a group of very influential individuals extending across national borders, dedicated to a new ordering of society. Some historians believe, for example, that they played a key role in the French Revolution."

"I thought that was a populist movement," Mason remarked, "aimed at overthrowing the monarchy and the aristocracy, the so-called Ancien Régime."

"By no means," Dieter Lutz countered. "Support for revolution permeated all levels of French society, at least in the early stages, before the onset of the Terror. Aristocrats wanted to wrest more power from the king and secure a meaningful role in government. The middle classes – prosperous merchants and members of the leading professions - also demanded a stronger say in running the country. The peasantry, for their part, chiefly aimed to abolish the onerous tithes and taxes which left them barely enough to support themselves and their families."

"Then how was it that so many aristocrats ended up as guests of Madame Guillotine?" his visitor asked.

The bookseller could not help but smile at his visitor's turn of phrase.

"Because some of them continued to support the Ancien Regime, either secretly or openly," he explained. "They were counting on Austrian and Prussian armies to invade France and crush the revolution in its infancy. Marie-Antoinette was, after all, an Austrian princess, the daughter of Empress Maria-Theresa."

George Mason was much impressed by the breadth of the Lutz's knowledge, but he still remained skeptical.

"I take your point about the aristos," he said. "And you may well be correct about the role of these people you call the Illuminati in the French Revolution. But what possible relevance could an organization like that have today?"

"Their aims and methods are secretive," came the considered reply. "But at a shrewd guess, I should say that they aim to infiltrate their members into key positions of power, as a first step to implementing their programs. No one would know in advance what those programs were. They may, in fact, already be well-advanced."

"You are implying," his visitor said, trying to get his head round this intriguing new concept, "that various U.N. agencies, to take just one example, may already have been penetrated at the highest level. Or such organizations as the World Bank and the International Monetary Fund?"

"Exactly," Dieter Lutz replied. "And do not forget the boardrooms of multinational companies, whose tentacles have a global reach."

"The Potenti would need to have considerable manpower to cover all those areas," Mason objected. "How then could it remain a secret society?"

"Have it your own way, Inspector Mason," Lutz replied, rather petulantly, while taking up his salami roll again. "Neither you nor I, in any event, is likely to have any bearing whatsoever on their objectives, whatever those may be. You have the information you requested, in so far as I am able to provide it. Is there anything else I can assist you with? Can I interest you, for example, in a rare book? We have an excellent selection."

"I shall call back before I leave town," the detective said, "to get some reading matter for the journey to Innsbruck."

"*Aufwiedersehen* then, *mein gute Herr*," the antiquarian said, affable again now that a sale was in prospect, as he unlocked the shop door to let his visitor out.

George Mason exited and made his way towards the far end of Schipfe, where it issued in a broad square fronted on three sides by a medieval guildhall, a row of elegant shops and the austere lines of the Fraumunster, a church that sheltered Huguenots fleeing religious persecution in France after the revocation of the Edict of Nantes in 1685. The fourth side was open to the river, where he lingered long enough to consume a bratwurst-with-mustard, freshly grilled by a street vendor. He enjoyed this makeshift lunch perched on the low embankment wall, watching the river traffic and the tourist launches. Approached by a Chinese couple to take their photograph beside a stone fountain playing in the center of the square, he was quite happy to oblige, wondering if Chinese tourists, increasingly prosperous nowadays, would soon outnumber Japanese visitors.

After his brief snack, he followed the river to its point of exit from the lake, crossed the bridge and continued along the strand, where he eventually located the British Consulate, housed in an elegant Victorian mansion facing the water. His enquiries there produced no indication that a Leonard Parks had contacted them in the event of personal difficulty. The consul was pleased that the detective had dropped by, noting with concern that a Briton was presumed missing somewhere between Zurich and Budapest and promising to be on the alert for possible developments. Mason had no luck either at police headquarters, the Polizei Dienst. According to Leutnant Rudi Kubler, who carefully checked his records, no Briton they were aware of had suffered an accident, for example, or fallen victim to foul play in recent weeks, apart from a Cambridge University student mugged late one night on the Niederdorf, the locus of the city's nightlife. Leutnant Kubler also contacted the local morgue on Mason's behalf, but again the result was negative. Personal documents and other objects retrieved from victims of traffic accidents and sundry misadventures showed no bearing on the case in hand, leaving the English detective reasonably convinced that the missing tax investigator had left Zurich in one piece, as he had done at Ostend, in order to contact the next individual on his tax-dodgers list.

CHAPTER FOUR

George Mason returned to his hotel in time to relax a little and freshen up before meeting up with Alison Aubrey. At just turned six o'clock on a fine late-summer evening, he went down to the foyer and found the young sergeant eagerly awaiting him, keen to see more of this fascinating city.

"I trust you have settled in all right?" he politely enquired.

"I just love my room," she replied. "They put fresh flowers and a bottle of mineral water on the bedside table. Very thoughtful of the hotel management. I also paid a quick visit to Bahnhofstrasse, to do some personal shopping."

"Glad to see you feel at home in the city," her colleague remarked. "If you are ready for dinner, there is a popular restaurant just across the river I thought we might try."

"Exploring Zurich on foot has sharpened my appetite," Alison said. "I can use a good meal."

Saying that, she fell in step beside him as they made their way towards the Wasserkirche, to cross the nearest bridge over the Limmat. Within minutes they reached Munsterhof, where George Mason had earlier taken his snack lunch, continuing along one of the narrow streets on its farther side to reach Zeughaus Keller. Descending the short flight of steps from street-level to access the spacious premises, they were greeted by a hostess clad in dirndl, who showed them to one of the few vacant tables.

"This is a popular place with Zurchers, as well as with tourists," Mason remarked, glancing round him. "It serves traditional Swiss fare, according to my guidebook."

"I am all for that," Alison commented, adding: "And this must be the largest restaurant I have ever visited."

"Cavernous, isn't it?" Mason said. "Explained by the fact these cellars once housed the city's main arsenal. That is the meaning of *Zeughaus*."

"Which adds an intriguing historical flavor," an impressed Alison Aubrey remarked, taking up the menu and puckering her brows at the unfamiliar items.

"I can recommend schnitzel with roesti," her companion helpfully suggested.

"Schnitzel will be veal," the young sergeant said. "But I have no idea what roesti is."

"It is as Swiss as it gets, Alison," came the reply. "Perhaps it could best be described as a sort of sautéed mashed potatoes. Delicious, when freshly prepared with chives."

"I shall take your word for it, George," she smilingly replied.

Mason ordered the same for both of them, with a half-carafe of wine from the Valais region, pleased that his companion seemed to be enjoying his choice of venue.

"Now tell me," he said, as they awaited service, "exactly how much you already know about the Parks case."

"Very little," she candidly replied, "apart from the fact that it concerns a missing person. Superintendent Maitland dropped this on me at very short notice and I jumped at the chance, for the experience it promised. He said that you would fill me in on the details."

"The individual in question," her colleague explained, "is a British tax investigator of Hungarian descent. Normally, such a matter would be left to the local police force, which in this case would be the Yorkshire Constabulary. But it seems that the Home Office is taking a strong interest. They especially requested Scotland Yard's involvement."

"So what have you come up with so far?" Alison wanted to know.

"Not very much, I am afraid, to be perfectly honest," he replied. "But it is early days yet."

The young woman's hazel eyes appraised him carefully, wondering if he was leveling with her. Could someone of George Mason's reputation really be as stumped as he seemed to be implying?

"Have you ruled out murder?" she enquired.

"I haven't ruled out anything," he replied. "I've already interviewed two of the people Leonard Parks was pursuing for back taxes. Neither of them struck me as likely assassins."

"What makes you so sure?"

"The first candidate, Colin Sutton, is a sommelier at one of Ostend's leading hotels, a bon viveur if ever there was one. He travels a lot, to wine tastings, conferences, auctions and the like. More to the point, he fully accepted his tax liabilities and has agreed to settle with the Inland Revenue. He would have no reason to harm Mr. Parks."

"And the other candidate?" an attentive Alison Aubrey asked.

"Dieter Lutz lives right here in Zurich," Mason explained. "I visited him earlier today in his bookshop at

Schipfe, a fascinating riverside arcade. He has moved permanently to Switzerland and now enjoys Swiss citizenship. He could not give a fig for any tax due to the Inland Revenue in England, which arose apparently from a large capital gain on the sale of his London property. Mainly as a gesture of goodwill, he offered a nominal sum in settlement."

"Which Leonard Parks accepted?"

"Parks was supposed to take the offer back to his superiors at Manchester for further consideration."

"So we can rule out Dieter Lutz as a possible suspect?"

"I should think so. He was, in fact, quite helpful in a way," Mason said, producing Parks' diary and passing it across the table, just as the waiter served their meal.

Alison placed it to one side to peruse later, as they both tackled their generous portions. The schnitzels were lightly battered and pan-fried, complemented by the golden-brown roesti. George Mason filled their wine glasses and proposed a toast to the success of their mission. Conversation lapsed for a while as they concentrated on their food, accompanied by the hum of activity from the nearby tables, one of which was occupied by a lively group of Chinese tourists.

"Quite appetizing," Alison remarked, at length nudging her plate aside with a smile of satisfaction. "I must look up a recipe for roesti when I get back home."

"I thought you would enjoy it," her colleague said, sipping his wine.

The young sergeant then turned her attention to Leonard Parks' pocket diary, flicking through the pages at random.

"Am I supposed to be looking for something in particular?" she asked.

"Look at the letters F.M.P. in the personal details," Mason prompted, without mentioning Dieter Lutz's theory, on the off-chance that Alison might come up with a different interpretation. "Do they mean anything to you?"

"Could be somebody's initials," she suggested. "P could stand for Parks, or possibly for one of his relatives."

"A possibility, Alison," her senior agreed. "The other items on that page all refer to Leonard Parks himself. His national insurance number, relevant phone numbers, date of birth, next of kin, and so on. These are not his wife's initials. Her forename is Justine."

"His mother's name then?" Alison suggested, tilting her wine glass towards him for a refill.

"Look at the list of phone numbers at the back of the diary," George Mason prompted. "Do you notice a Léni Farkas?"

Alison did as instructed, scanning the page and glancing questioningly at her colleague.

"Léni Farkas is Leonard's mother," he informed her.

"You *have* been doing your homework, George," his colleague remarked, appreciatively. "But how would you know something like that?"

"Justine Parks told me that her husband's original family name was Farkas. He anglicized it to Parks when he moved to England following his marriage. I reasoned that Léni Farkas had to be a close relative, either his mother, an unmarried sister or a paternal aunt. I rang the number this very afternoon. It is his mother all right."

"Did her son contact her on his recent visit here?"

"That is what we are about to find out, as soon as we finished dinner. We are going to visit her at her home around eight o'clock."

"Then we had better get a move on," Alison said, checking her watch. "It is already turned seven."

"A quick coffee, and I shall settle the bill," Mason said.

"Léni Farkas does not live very far from here. I found her address on a street map. We have sufficient time."

Twenty minutes later, having rounded off their meal, the two detectives stood waiting in encroaching dusk at the No.15 tram stop on Limmatquai, watching a tourist launch tie up for the night at the opposite embankment, within earshot of dance music from the garden restaurant farther upstream.

"Sounds like someone is having fun," Alison said, tapping her foot in time to the music.

"Young couples, mainly, I should think," Mason replied, "taking advantage of a fine evening."

"Will you be able to find this address all right, George?" Alison anxiously enquired, as the two-car tram came to a halt on the central reservation. "It will be quite dark in a little while."

"Léni Farkas lives in an apartment house directly opposite Bahnhof Oerlikon, which also happens to be the tram terminus," George Mason replied, unconcerned. "No. 26, Windstrasse, to be precise. I doubt we can miss it."

The automatic doors clanked shut, as the tram sped a short distance alongside the river before stopping again at the large interchange near the Hauptbahnhof, to set down a few rail passengers. It then accelerated in a westerly direction towards the commercial suburb of Oerlikon, now shrouded in darkness, its offices and shops shuttered for the night. On alighting, they crossed the street and soon located the apartment house, taking the lift to the third floor, where they rang the doorbell against the name Farkas. It was some time before their summons was answered, but eventually they heard a shuffling of feet approaching the door. It opened slowly on a chain, as an elderly woman with a pronounced stoop peered cautiously out.

"George Mason," the detective announced. "I telephoned earlier today."

The occupant freed the chain and opened the door wider, seemingly reassured by the additional presence of a young woman.

"Please step in, Mr. Mason," she said, securing the door behind them. "I have been expecting you."

With that, she led the way into a dimly-lit living-room with heavy old-fashioned furniture, inviting them to sit.

"You said on the phone that you knew my son Leonard," Léni Farkas began. "So what is all this about?"

"Your son was, I believe, in Zurich approximately two weeks ago," George Mason replied. "Did he visit you on that occasion?"

"Leonard always visits his mother when he has business in Switzerland," the woman proudly asserted. "But that situation does not arise very often, certainly not as often as I should like."

The detective took that as an affirmative, while casting about in his mind how best to break the news that her son had gone missing. He decided to come straight to the point.

"Detective Sergeant Aubrey and I," he said, with a glance towards his colleague, "have come here from London. Your son has not contacted either his wife Justine or his head office in Manchester since he left England."

On hearing that, Léni Farkas looked a little aggrieved, but not unduly surprised.

"Leonard always gets very involved in his work," she said. "I expect he has simply been too preoccupied."

"Has he contacted you since you saw him last?" Alison Aubrey asked.

The woman firmly shook her head.

"Do you happen to know where your son was headed

after taking his leave of you?" Mason asked.

"I think he intended to visit Glarus," Léni Farkas said, rather guardedly. "That is a mountain resort in the eastern part of the country. His father Laszlo is buried there, in the graveyard of the Priory of St. Kasimir."

"Your husband?" Alison prompted.

Léni nodded, her wrinkled features assuming a wistful expression.

"Laszlo was devoted to the priory," she said. "In the old days, he was Count Laszlo Farkas, but he was stripped of his title after the war, when the Communists took control of Eastern Europe. But he retained many influential friends in the old European aristocracy, many of whom had already moved to France or Switzerland, as safe havens. St. Kasimir's was a focal point for their bi-annual reunions. The monks looked after them very well in their guesthouse and, I am sure, received generous donations in return."

"Tell me," a much-intrigued George Mason said, "do the letters F.M.P. mean something to you?"

Léni Farkas smilingly shook her head.

"I came across them countless times," she said, "on Laszlo's personal stationery.   But you must understand, Mr. Mason, that women of my generation did not pry very closely into their husbands' affairs. It was not our place to do so. Our main role was to produce heirs to the great estates and to supervise the servants and the domestic arrangements. A good life it was, while it still existed. But where are those landed properties now? Long since confiscated by the Communists, in the name of social leveling."

The two detectives exchanged smiles at her rueful remarks, George Mason reflecting how differently things had turned out in England, where the aristocracy was still very much in place, even if their assets had been depleted in recent decades by inheritance taxes. Many stately homes, too large to be adequately maintained, had been razed to the ground.

"In England," she continued, as if reading his thoughts, "you have retained respect for the higher social orders. Look at your House of Lords, for example, a key component of your Parliament, with an effective voice in the political process. Where else in the Europe of today is there anything remotely comparable?"

"That is very true," Sergeant Aubrey chipped in. "But the main power resides in the House of Commons. There are relatively few hereditary peers left, most of the current members of the upper house being appointed for life, in recognition of their public service. Anglican bishops also have seats in the House of Lords."

"The Farkas family were always great admirers of the English system," Léni continued. "How you could adapt historic institutions, such as your monarchy, to suit modern conditions, without sweeping everything away in violent revolutions and starting over from scratch. You have an enviable continuity with your past. Leonard was more than happy to make his life in England, on marrying Justine. I shall ring her after you have left, to inform her of your visit."

"Why not call her straight away," Mason suggested, thinking there was at least a possibility that the tax investigator might in the meantime have contacted his wife, in which case a deal of time and trouble would be saved.

"First, you must let me offer you both a glass of the Hungarian schnapps," she replied, rising unsteadily to her feet and slowly wheeling a small trolley holding a decanter and crystal glasses into the center of the room. With no lack of ceremony, she measured out generous tots for the three of them.

"To your good health," the detective said, raising his glass.

"To your most dutiful queen," Léni proposed. "Long may she reign!"

Toasts completed, she picked up the phone and rang Balderstones.

"Justine, my dear," she began, as the line became live. "I have with me here a Mr. George Mason from Scotland Yard, who claims that Leonard has not contacted either you or the Revenue people since he left England. This is all quite perplexing, but you know how absent-minded he can be. Have you by any chance heard from him in the last few days?"

George Mason could tell from her expression that the answer was negative. After a few brief exchanges about personal matters, she handed him the receiver.

"Justine," the detective said. "How are things with you?"

"I am bearing up," she replied.

"Good. Now listen carefully, Justine. We have traced your husband as far as Zurich. So far, so good. No indications of anything untoward happening to him. His meetings with two tax clients, Sutton and Lutz, all apparently went smoothly and according to plan. There is no cause for alarm."

"I am very relieved to hear that, Inspector," Justine replied. "I feel sure you will do your utmost on our behalf. Do please keep me informed as your enquiries progress."

"I shall do that," he assured her. "Good night, Justine, and take care."

After another half-hour of interesting conversation with their hostess about her life in Zurich, the detectives drained their glasses, rose from their chairs and moved towards the door.

"I do not think we need take up more of your time," George Mason remarked, "as it is getting quite late. Thank you so much for agreeing to meet with us, Mrs. Farkas, and for sharing with us something of your fascinating family history."

"Do not mention it, Herr Mason," Léni Farkas said. "Please let me know at once of any developments. You have my phone number."

Sitting in the tram, as it picked up speed back towards the Limmatquai and Hotel Adler, Mason remarked to his young colleague:

"Of course, we shall now be obliged to visit Glarus, Alison, even though it was not one of Leonard Parks' scheduled calls."

"Leave no stone unturned, George?"

"We cannot afford to in an investigation like this. Wherever Leonard Parks went, we must go too, in case we miss some vital clue to his present whereabouts. I suggest we leave first thing tomorrow morning, immediately after breakfast."

"At least we shall see more of the Swiss alps," Alison commented. "Where precisely is Glarus?"

"It is over towards the Austrian border," came the reply. "Just over an hour by train from here."

*

George Mason woke very early the following morning. Since it was clear weather, he took a stroll along the Limmat embankment to kill time before the hotel restaurant opened at seven. A few early commuters were about, as the gulls wheeled noisily overhead, darting low towards the water or strutting along the sidewalks seeking scraps of food. He was already at table, enjoying his first coffee while scanning the local newspaper, *Tages Anzeiger,* when Detective Sergeant Alison Aubrey joined him, clad in a light anorak and denim skirt. They ordered a typical Swiss breakfast of muesli, with yoghurt and fresh fruit. An hour later, they set off towards the Hauptbahnhof, where they took the train to Ziegelbrucke. It was a local service, calling at the affluent lakeside suburbs of Kusnacht and Thalwil on the way.

"Isn't it something, George," his colleague remarked, "to be traveling right into the heart of the country?"

"Indeed, Alison," he replied. "And you shall know we are in the alps when we ride the cog railway from Ziegelbrucke to Glarus. They need the third rail to climb the steep gradient."

"Are we going so high?" she asked.

"The highest peak in the area is Todi," Mason explained. "Closely followed by Glarnisch. The town of Glarus is situated close to the Wallensee, the deepest lake in Switzerland. According to my guidebook, which I read before retiring last night, Canton Glarus is noted mainly for forestry, dairy farming and hydro-electricity. It is also one of the few cantons to have retained direct democracy."

"What exactly does that mean?" Alison prompted.

"It means that, instead of electing representatives to pass laws and raise taxes, as in the British Parliament or the American Congress, all inhabitants vote in open assembly, in what is known as the Landesgemeinde, to approve or reject all proposals for new legislation and sources of revenue."

"The other cantons don't do likewise?" Alison asked, in

some surprise.

"They also have direct democracy," Mason replied, "with the key difference that all voting takes place by secret ballot."

"Glarus has what I would call genuine democracy," Alison remarked, with conviction. "Who knows when our members of Parliament, for example, are not voting for vested interests, or under pressure from lobbyists?"

"It sounds ideal, I agree," her companion said. "But it would only work with relatively small populations. How could all the inhabitants of an English county or an American state get together in one open assembly? It is just not practicable."

"I take your point," she rejoined, as the train pulled into Ziegelbrucke.

"This is where we change trains," Mason said, rising from his seat and leading the way to the exit.

On reaching the waiting-room, George Mason quickly consulted the timetable, the *Fahrplan*. They then crossed a footbridge to reach a different platform, where the connection to Glarus was already waiting. Clambering aboard, they found seats in a carriage that soon filled up with tourists. Mason quickly identified them as French or German, plus a few Swiss hikers in lederhosen heading for the mountain trails. After running on level ground for a few miles, the vintage steam locomotive commenced its slow, labored climb up the steep gradient, affording spectacular views on either hand. After an exhilarating trip lasting just under an hour, it set them down near the center of Glarus.

George Mason enquired of the station master the quickest way to the Priory of St. Kasimir. Giving the detective an odd look, the official waved his arm in the general direction of a forested hillside overlooking the

Wallensee.

"It is a fair walk," the man said, in German, glancing dubiously at the portly figure facing him.

"And a nice day for it, too," Mason replied, leading the way out of the station and along the main street of the compact alpine town, pointing out as they went the colorful murals on the facades of the buildings.

Emerging at the far end of the main street into open country, they soon noticed a weathered sign indicating the path up to the priory. It was so narrow that they had to proceed in single file, Alison Aubrey taking the lead until they came to a bench part-way up the slope, so positioned as to gain full advantage of the view across Switzerland's deepest lake. They sat down momentarily to catch their breath.

"Quite amazingly beautiful," Alison said, squatting down beside him. "Look how blue the water is. I am almost tempted to take a swim."

"You would find it pretty chilly," the detective said, "even at this time of year. Throughout the winter, it will have been covered with several feet of ice."

"Hard to imagine, looking at it now," she remarked. "How much farther to climb, George? You look a little beat already. Mind you don't overdo it."

George Mason smiled to himself at her concern, while rising gingerly to his feet.

"You'd think they would install a chairlift, or even a cable car," he ironically remarked.

"I expect the monks prefer to deter, rather than encourage, visitors," came Alison's perceptive reply.

"That may well be the case," he agreed, putting his best foot forward while avoiding being snagged by the brambles that strayed across the path. Alison, he felt, had made a valid point, if this was the only way up to the priory.

Some twenty minutes later, they came to a large clearing before a low, rambling building built back into the hillside, with small turrets placed at intervals across the pantile roofs. Mason figured that it was not originally meant as a monastery, being more likely the home of a local grandee of some bygone century, well before the era of direct democracy at the Glarus Landesgemeinde. To the left, higher up the slope and fringed with pine trees, he spotted the graveyard that Léni Farkas had mentioned last evening. There being no sign of human presence on the outside, the Scotland Yard pair approached what they took to be the main entrance and yanked a metal bell-pull beside the door. There was no response, even though they heard a bell sounding from deep inside the premises. Mason took a few steps backwards and glanced up at the leaded windows, with a puzzled glance towards his colleague.

This time, Alison Aubrey gave the bell-pull two more tugs in quick succession. There soon followed the sound of heavy bolts being drawn back behind the heavy oaken door, which then opened just a few inches. An elderly monk with wispy white hair peered closely at them.

"What is it that you seek?" he asked, in German.

"I wish to speak with the prior," Mason said, "if that would be possible."

"If it is alms you are seeking," the monk said, rather impatiently, "go to the side entrance and report to the almoner."

The detective was mortified to think that he looked like a beggar, while Alison could hardly suppress a smile of amusement.

"I wish to speak with the prior on a matter of some urgency," he retorted. "It has nothing to do with alms."

The heavy door opened a little wider, allowing the monk a closer appraisal of Mason's companion.

"No woman may set foot inside St. Kasimir's," he said. "But you, sir, if you so desire, may enter briefly while I consult with our superior."

Mason glanced ruefully at his colleague. She in turn glanced smilingly from him to the monk, soon realizing, however, that feminine charm was not going to move mountains. She turned away and made as if to head back down the sloping path.

"Tell you what," Mason said, encouragingly. "While I am inside the priory, which I do not imagine will be for very long given the level of welcome, why don't you take a look round the graveyard and see if you can locate the burial plot of Count Laszlo Farkas? You could wait for me just outside this door afterwards."

As the young sergeant headed towards the far side of the priory, the elderly monk opened the door just wide enough to permit the visitor to enter, leading the way across a stone-floored entrance hall to a room at the far end.

"Be pleased to wait here, Mr.…?" he said.

"Mason," he replied at once. "George Mason, from London." He purposely did not give his official title.

The sound of the octogenarian's surprisingly sprightly footsteps receded across the hall, leaving the visitor to take in his surroundings. The room contained a minimum of furniture, just a bare wooden table and four straight-backed chairs. The sole decorative features were a small icon representing an archangel and what Mason took to be a coat-of-arms. Moving closer to examine the latter, he found that it showed a sinewy forearm clutching an uprooted tree with bare branches. Most likely, he thought, it was the escutcheon of a former occupant of the building, possibly one of those medieval Swiss counts forever defending their turf against Austrian incursions. Until he made out the rather faded motto beneath it. It read *Faciant Meliora Potentes*! Assuming that Dieter Lutz's explanation of the Latin was correct, that it was the adopted motto of a secret society called the Potenti, the implication seemed inescapable that St. Kasimir's Priory was connected with it! How amazing was that, he thought.

"Very effective, isn't it, Herr Mason?"

The detective spun round on his heels, to be confronted by a balding, but still quite young-looking individual clad in a long white robe with a dark-brown hood, whom he took to be the prior.

"An interesting motto, certainly," George Mason replied, accepting the offer of a seat on one of the hard monastic chairs.

"You understand Latin?" the other asked, in pleasant surprise.

"Let those who can do better," Mason offered, as a fair translation.

"Quite so, Herr Mason," the prior said. "But you did not climb all this way up the bramble path to decipher Latin mottos?"

"Actually," his visitor said, "I am trying to trace an acquaintance of mine from England. I believe, from speaking with his mother, that he may have visited this priory quite recently."

"You are referring, no doubt, to our dear son, Leonard Farkas," the prior said, referring to the tax investigator by his original family name. "Indeed, he was here two weeks or so ago, to place fresh flowers on his father's grave. The old count was a notable benefactor to our ancient foundation. He expressed the wish to be buried here, among good friends, a wish we were only too happy to grant."

George Mason thought he had better come straight to the point.

"Leonard Parks, or Farkas if you wish, has gone missing," he explained. "I am hoping you can perhaps give me some pointers to his present whereabouts."

The prior weighed his visitor's remarks carefully, before gravely shaking his tonsured head.

"I am sorry to hear that Leonard may be in some difficulty," he said. "But I do not see how I can be of very much assistance to you. Our life here is very secluded. We are an enclosed order with a strict vow of silence. We rarely venture beyond the confines of St. Kasimir's."

"Yet you say he paid a visit here?"

"As an act of filial devotion to his father's memory," the other replied. "Of course, we invited him in for some light refreshment and chatted about this and that, mainly about old times. He seemed quite his usual self and very content with his present circumstances in England. Are you now implying that he has met with some sort of misadventure?"

"That remains to be determined," the detective replied. "Did he show any signs of anxiety or misgivings while in your company?"

"None whatsoever," came the reply. "Quite the opposite, in fact. He was dedicated to his work for the Inland Revenue and briefly referred to successful outcomes of his enquiries at Ostend and Zurich. As to his personal affairs, he struck me as devoted to his wife Justine, whom he met on a Danube cruise."

The detective's gaze returned involuntarily to the escutcheon on the far wall, something that did not escape the prior's notice.

"About what time of day did he leave St. Kasimir's?" Mason then asked.

"In the early evening," the prior confirmed. "Moments before our small community repaired to the chapel to sing Vespers. He was intending to return to Zurich and stay overnight at Hotel Adler. The following day, I believe he was heading to the Innsbruck area."

"Or perhaps to the Tyrol?" Mason prompted.

"Which lies to the south of Innsbruck, I do believe."

"Much obliged to you, Father...?" the detective said, rising to his feet.

"Dominic," the prior replied, stepping deftly aside to let his visitor exit the room ahead of him. "I am at your service, Sir. If there is any way we can assist you further in this matter, do not hesitate to contact me. We are connected to the telephone system, one of our few concessions to modernity. Now, if you will excuse me, I must get back to my study to prepare a homily."

George Mason thought it unlikely that he would get much more out of the reclusive prior. Emerging from the building and glancing round for a sign of his colleague, he considered the detour to the eastern alps very worthwhile, in that it seemed to establish a link between St. Kasimir's and the Potenti. And it was beginning to seem to him that, like father like son, Leonard Parks, né Farkas, might also be a member of this mysterious group; hence his use of the monogram F.M.P. on his personal stationery and computer files. Heading in the direction of the cemetery, he at length caught up with Alison Aubrey, before leading the way back down the narrow, overgrown path, a trek far easier than the ascent.

"It is nearly two o'clock," he remarked, when they regained the outskirts of the town. "Time for a spot of lunch, eh, Alison?"

"I am quite ravenous," she replied, "after all this exercise in the mountain air. Let us find a comfortable inn, not too crowded."

Proceeding along the main street of Glarus, mingling with the tourists, they eventually came to an establishment called Der Goldener Hirsch. George Mason briefly studied the menu posted on the outside wall, a practice common to Swiss restaurants. He liked what he saw and led the way in.

"How does raclettes strike you?" he enquired of his companion, the moment they were seated at the bare pinewood table. "It is the house specialty, apparently, and typically Swiss."

"I could eat almost anything at this point," she replied. "If you recommend it, let us place an order without delay."

A waiter soon appeared and took their order for raclettes and two steins of beer. It being past the normal lunch-hour, only a handful of customers lingered over wine or coffee. The pair did not anticipate a long wait for service. Earthenware steins of the local brew quickly arrived. Fifteen minutes later, they watched with keen interest as the waiter placed a dish of boiled potatoes and mixed vegetables before them. He returned with a large Emmental cheese tucked securely under his left arm. Holding a heated knife in his right hand, he commenced peeling thin slices off it, which immediately melted on contact with the warm food.

"*Guten appetit*," he said with a cheery smile, his task completed.

After sampling the tasty dish in silence for a while, George Mason said:

"Did you find much of interest up there at the priory?"

"You mean apart from the grave of Laszlo Farkas?"

Her colleague nodded.

"Some of the graves close to the count's," Alison said, "seemed to belong to German officers."

"S.S. or Wehrmacht?" he enquired, keenly interested.

"What is the difference?"

"The S.S. were the elite Nazi troops, Alison. S.S. is short for *Schutzstaffel*. The Wehrmacht were the regular army, some of whose officers actually opposed Adolf Hitler and his whole agenda."

"I saw no indication that they might have been S.S.," Alison said, intrigued at his explanation. "No Nazi insignia on the headstones, for instance. But I wasn't specially looking for things like that."

"They may not have wished to advertise the fact," Mason remarked. "Whoever they were, they most likely fled across the border with Switzerland in the closing stages of World War 11. There would have been individuals, sympathizers in the German-speaking cantons, willing to help them do that. That is possibly how so many Nazis eventually made their way to South America."

"But why would some be lying in St. Kasimir's graveyard?" Alison wondered.

"At a shrewd guess," he replied, "they had close connections with the priory, through membership of a secret society known as the Potenti."

The younger officer returned an astonished look, while forking the last mouthful of raclettes before nudging her plate aside.

"How on earth would you know something like that, George?" she asked.

Mason's features broke into a broad conspiratorial grin, but he continued eating for a while until he had consumed all but a small portion of the food. With a sigh of satisfaction, he too set his plate aside and took a quaff of beer.

"My word," he remarked. "What an appetizing dish! A specialty, I believe, of the French-speaking cantons. All the more surprising to find it served here in Glarus."

"Perhaps the chef is from the Jura," Alison suggested. "But you have not answered my question."

"It is all down to the monogram F.M.P.," he explained. "Léni Farkas mentioned that her husband, Count Farkas, used it on all personal documents, and that he visited the priory at least twice a year for reunions. While inside the priory, I noticed a coat-of-arms on the wall, with the Latin motto *Faciant Meliora Potentes.*"

"And I thought they were somebody's initials," an intrigued Alison Aubrey remarked.

"A fair enough guess, in the circumstances," her colleague generously allowed. "But it was, in fact, the antiquarian bookseller, Dieter Lutz, who first alerted me to their significance. I am due to pay him a return visit at his premises on Schipfe, just across the river from our hotel."

"Exactly who are these people?" a deeply-curious Alison enquired.

"That is something I myself would very much like to learn," he replied. "I have a shrewd idea that Leonard Parks may have been involved with them, since he too used the same monogram, except that below it he also had the words *Semper Diligens.*"

"Which mean?"

"Always watchful, I suppose, would be a fair translation."

"How fascinating," Alison remarked. "Kudos to you, George, for your knowledge of Latin."

Mason was content to bathe for a few moments in his

sergeant's high regard. He raised his beer stein and proposed a light-hearted toast:

"To the Potenti," he said. "Whoever, and wherever, they may be."

"The Potenti," Alison chimed in, sharing her senior's jocular mood.

At that point, the innkeeper approached their table to enquire how they had enjoyed their meal.

"Quite excellent," Mason said, with conviction.

"And what brings you to Glarus?" the innkeeper asked, not viewing them as typical tourists.

"To visit the local priory," Alison replied.

The man's ruddy features registered a degree of surprise.

"At this time of year?" he asked.

"Why do you ask?" returned the detective.

"St. Kasimir's usually receives visitors only twice a year. The monks are members of a contemplative order who rarely engage with the general public."

"So when do they permit themselves to open up, as it were?" Alison wanted to know. "To actually suspend their vow of silence and speak to people?"

"In mid-May and mid-November," came the reply. "A fair number of important people converge on Glarus at those times. Quite often they use my humble establishment for overflow accommodation, since the priory guesthouse can only take so many. They also sometimes have informal get-togethers here. Drinks round the bar, usually, after their formal dinners."

"Do you happen to know who these notable guests are?" an immediately curious George Mason enquired.

"All I can tell you is that they come from across Europe," the innkeeper explained. "Even from England, I do believe. I have no idea what their business is at the priory, but I have recognized over the years several prominent European Union officials, for example."

"Must be top-level discussions," the detective remarked. "Something like the G8 annual forum of world leaders. I would give half my pension to know what they are about."

The innkeeper returned a curiously skeptical smile.

"Take it from me, *mein gute Herr,*" he said, "that is something you will never find out. Not unless you are invited there yourself. I have been speculating on the character of those meetings for a number of years, without becoming any the wiser, even after overhearing snatches of bar conversation."

George Mason reacted to that admission in some surprise.

"I expect you are right about that," he resignedly admitted, extracting his wallet to settle the bill.

"Forty-five francs even," the innkeeper said.

The detective gave him a fifty-franc note, to include a tip for the waiter, and rose to his feet. Alison Aubrey paid a quick visit to the restroom and soon rejoined her colleague in the lively street outside.

CHAPTER FIVE

It was a rather overcast evening in early September when Sir Maurice Weeks, First Secretary at the Exchequer, drove his Bentley from his Mayfair address to the Royal Hunt Hotel at Putney Bridge, some miles south of the River Thames. On arrival there, he parked his car and walked smartly towards the premises, heading through the lobby to a small conference room at the rear, where he joined a select group of individuals drawn from the highest ranks of government and commerce. Taking his customary place at the head of the table, he exchanged cordial greetings with them before getting down to the business in hand.

"Sorry to keep you waiting," he began, aware that he was about ten minutes behind schedule. "Unforeseen circumstances, I am afraid."

"We are not quite a quorum, Sir Maurice," Edmond Brierley, the person on his immediate left, said. "One of our number had a prior commitment."

The civil servant dismissed the objection.

"We are simply in the planning stages, Edmond," he said. "We shall need the full quorum only when the occasion arises to make firm decisions, which must be by majority vote."

"Did you call this meeting," Arthur Teesdale, who sat

facing him, enquired, "with regard to the upcoming vacancy at the head of the International Monetary Fund?"

"Indeed I did," Weeks replied. "And it is of vital importance that we install one of our own people as the new director. As you know, the Fund was established to provide aid to economies in difficulties, to ensure global financial stability."

"Which it has largely succeeded in doing, Sir Maurice," Brierley commented, "in Latin America particularly in recent years. Globalization implies that problems in one country will spill over into another, with a domino effect, risking world-wide recession."

"We need to radically reform the way the Fund operates," Weeks said, "so that it does not become a constant drain on the taxpayer. I.M.F loans have notably escalated over the last several years, with no firm prospect of their being fully repaid."

"What specific measures do you have in mind, Sir Maurice?" a rather skeptical Edmond Brierley asked.

The Exchequer official poured himself a glass of mineral water from the dispenser, leaned back expansively in his chair and said:

"As you are well aware, the current method of financing the Fund's operations is for each member country, depending on its gross national product, to pay an appropriate quota. I propose tapping into global bond markets instead, to provide loans of short-term duration."

"Isn't there then the risk that countries will default on their national debt?" Arthur Teesdale asked.

"In the event that a given country cannot pay its way," Weeks replied, "bondholders will have to take haircuts. In that way, governments of failing countries will be required to take drastic measures to ensure solvency. If they fail to do so, few investors will be motivated to buy their sovereign debt."

"By drastic measures" Edwina Cleary, the sole female present, said, "you mean increasing tax revenues and cutting back on welfare benefits, such as healthcare and social security?"

"Each country must put its own house in order, "the Exchequer official emphasized. "There is the danger that bailouts by the I.M.F. may promote a kind of moral hazard, in that some countries will be profligate in the full expectation that the international community will come to their aid."

"These are very radical proposals, Sir Maurice," Brierley remarked.

"Which is precisely why we need one of our own people to head the Fund," came the reply. "He or she can gradually steer members of the international executive committee round to our way of thinking."

"How does the World Bank fit into the overall picture?" Arthur Teesdale asked.

"They are mainly involved in development projects for third-world countries," the civil servant replied, "using a mixture of public and private loans and investment, backed by the latest technology and research. The president is invariably an American appointee, so we have little leverage on their policy decisions."

"We need to build up our presence in America," Edmond Brierley said. "What is the situation so far?'

"As I understand it," Sir Maurice informed him, "our society is in the early stages of making a meaningful presence in the U.S.A. So far, we have three congressmen on board, several prominent business leaders and two university professors. But we are working on it, to eventually increase our grip on world finances overall."

"Meanwhile," Edwina asked, "what are our associates in Europe doing?"

"They will use their influence to back our candidate for I.M.F. director," Weeks explained. "In addition to that, they have their hands full nominating one of their own people for the upcoming vacancy of Finance Commissioner at Brussels."

"If our people control finance at the European Commission," Teesdale said, "we will effectively control most other aspects of the Commission's work."

"The power of the purse," Edwina Cleary remarked, with satisfaction.

"Unfortunately," Sir Maurice said, "since Britain is exiting the European Union, we shall have to leave that little matter in the capable hands of our French and Irish friends. My counterpart at the Dublin treasury, Colm Byrne, will likely fit the bill."

"But Ireland is not in line to nominate a European Commissioner," Arthur Teesdale objected. "That privilege will fall to one of the East European countries that have recently joined the European Union."

The Exchequer official knit his brows, while considering the matter. The others waited expectantly on his answer.

"A bribe in the right quarters should do the trick," he said, matter-of-factly.

"It will take to be a very considerable sum," Edmond Brierley cautioned, "to achieve that objective. How will it be raised?"

"Our friends across the Channel have the matter well in hand," Sir Maurice replied. "You can take it from me that Colm Byrne will likely be the next financial supremo at Brussels."

"As I see it," Edwina Cleary said, to steer the conversation away from the delicate subject of bribery, "Byrne would be keen to phase out carbon permits. It was a big mistake to award them gratis to certain industries, instead of exacting a realistic price for them. They have simply become a license to pollute."

"I am confident the Irishman will tighten up the whole procedure," Sir Maurice informed them. "The Commissioners will no longer be able to yield to pressure from the extractive industries, or to special pleading from interest groups, including automobile manufacturers."

"It is sincerely to be hoped not," Arthur Teesdale said. "That policy has resulted in increased carbon emissions every year since it came into force. At least, renewable energy is on the march. Look at Denmark, a good example to all of us. The Danes hope to be carbon-neutral by 2025."

"More credit to them," Sir Maurice observed, approvingly. "Mark my words, all will change for the better, including revocation of other questionable measures recently pushed through by the bureaucrats at Brussels, as soon as our society fully controls the funds. I mean, do we really need limits on the volume of sound an orchestra can make?"

At that remark, sniggers of amusement ran through the small gathering, enlivened by Edmond Brierley's mimicking of a trombonist. Regaining seriousness, they discussed other key aspects of social policy, including immigration control and border security, before going down promptly at seven o'clock to the spacious lounge bar for aperitifs, followed at seven-thirty by a traditional dinner of Angus roast beef and Yorkshire pudding in the elegant dining-room.

*

On the evening following their side-trip to Glarus, George Mason and Alison Aubrey took their evening meal in the restaurant of Hotel Adler, hoping that the heavy rain would abate somewhat before they ventured outside. By seven o'clock, however, there was no sign of clearer skies, yet the inspector was keen to pay another visit to the antiquarian bookstore, which remained open until 8.00 p.m.

"It never occurred to me to bring along an umbrella," he remarked to his colleague, half apologetically.

"It did not occur to me either," Alison replied. "Leaving England and heading south, one tends to take fine weather for granted. A triumph of optimism, I suppose."

"In Switzerland, one has to take the alps into consideration," Mason commented. "They have a marked effect on the weather. All that warm air streaming across the Mediterranean from North Africa picks up a lot of moisture, bringing heavy downpours like this when it crosses the alps. Usually, however, they are of fairly short duration."

From their places at table, they watched the rain bounce back from the sidewalk and form rivulets in the gutters.

"Nothing for it but to take our chances," Mason said. "We cannot sit here all evening when there is work to be done."

"I am game, if you are," Alison Aubrey sportingly replied.

"If we keep close to the line of the buildings and cross the bridge by the Wasserkirche," he added, "we shall reach Schipfe in about ten minutes, where I intend to purchase a book for Bill Harrington. Or, if you prefer, you can remain here at table, order fresh coffee and read the newspaper until I get back."

"And miss all the fun, George?" she quipped. "More to the point, I do not read German."

"In that case, you should by all means come," George Mason encouragingly replied, rising from his place by the window.

Alison Aubrey returned briefly to her room to retrieve her anorak, then kept close to her senior as he led the way out of the hotel and veered left along the Limmatquai, ducking occasionally into shop doorways until they reached the bridge. There was a slight lull in the storm at this more exposed point, allowing them to gain the shelter of the covered arcade without getting too wet. Pausing for breath, they gazed momentarily at the raging torrent of the River Limmat, now empty of tourist traffic.

"Take a stroll along the arcade, Alison," Mason then suggested. "I am sure you will find the various craft boutiques of interest."

The young sergeant frowned a little at his decision to attend to his business alone. Superintendent Maitland had instructed her to be at Mason's side throughout the course of his enquiries and make careful note of his activities. But if this was merely a question of buying a book for the chief inspector, she reasoned that there could not be much harm in that. Besides, she loved arts and crafts, especially costume jewelry and ceramics. George Mason turned away and soon reached the bookstore, stepping inside to the melodious chime of the doorbell. The proprietor, Dieter Lutz, glanced up from his desk in the far corner, where he was engaged in updating his inventory.

"Herr Mason," he exclaimed, agreeably surprised. "You remembered to return, after all. You wish to make a purchase?"

"Provided it is not too expensive," the detective replied, conscious that he was already a little over-budget.

"I have the very thing," the bookseller said, turning to the shelves to collect a hardback edition with a slightly-torn dust jacket.

He handed it to his visitor, watching closely for his reaction.

"Thomas Mann?" an intrigued George Mason remarked. "At least, I have heard of him."

"*The Magic Mountain*," Lutz explained, "is considered by some authorities to be his finest work. One of the key novels of the twentieth century, in fact."

"How much are you asking?" his visitor asked.

"It is marked down," the other replied, "because it is not actually a first edition, but an early reprint. A first edition Thomas Mann would be very costly, but I can let you have this copy for a mere hundred francs."

The detective turned the book over in his grasp and pursed his lips, thoughtfully. He had little experience of the rare book market and did not wish to be taken for a ride.

"I shall certainly consider it," he said, postponing the decision to a later date, while thinking that Bill Harrington would surely appreciate it. The chief inspector, in addition to his taste for single-malt whiskies, had an extensive home library.

"Have you had any more thoughts on what we discussed at your last visit?" the bookseller then enquired.

"You are referring, no doubt, to the Potenti?" George Mason replied.

Dieter Lutz nodded expectantly.

"I may even have rubbed shoulders with them," the detective cryptically announced.

"The devil you don't say so!" the other exclaimed, his

eyes opening wide in astonishment, while taking a step closer to gauge his visitor's facial expression. Was his visitor being serious or jocular?

"I am all ears, Herr Mason," he said. "Do please explain yourself."

"Leonard Parks' mother, Léni, lives over in Oerlikon," the detective explained. "My colleague and I paid her a visit two days ago. She informed me that her husband, Count Laszlo Farkas, was a regular visitor to St. Kasimir's Priory and that his remains are interred in the graveyard there. She also told me that her son intended to visit the grave while he was in Switzerland."

"So off you went to Glarus?" the intrigued bookseller asked.

"Earlier today, as a matter of fact."

"But you surely did not rub shoulders with actual members of the Potenti?" Dieter Lutz countered.

George Mason smilingly shook his head and stepped to one side as a potential customer entered the premises and browsed among the bookshelves.

"Not in the literal sense," he admitted, out of the browser's earshot. "But I did form the impression that the priory is somehow connected with the Potenti and that, according to a local innkeeper, notable people gather there twice a year, some of whom take lodgings at his inn, Der Goldener Hirsch."

"What is so surprising about that?" Lutz asked. "Notable personalities, including politicians, business leaders and academics often gather in Swiss locales. Take the World Economic Forum, for example, the annual jamboree at Davos."

"In the reception room at St. Kasimir's," the detective continued, "where I met briefly with the prior, Father

Dominic, there is a coat of arms on the wall, with the motto *Faciant Meliora Potentes*! Count Farkas also had the monogram F.M.P. inscribed on his personal stationery. Putting two and two together, I should say that both the nobleman and his son were affiliated to the Potenti. And I am wondering if that may have some bearing on Leonard Parks' present whereabouts. Leni Farkas apparently knows nothing about a secret society, never having pried too closely into her husband's affairs."

"How enterprising of you, Herr Mason," the bookseller said, in admiration. "Now, I in turn have some news for you."

"Indeed?" rejoined the detective, expectantly.

"Since our last meeting, I have been in touch with a young man who is a distant relative of my wife. I was not going to mention this, since I could not vouch for its accuracy. But what you have just told me would seem to corroborate it."

"Corroborate what, Herr Lutz?" George Mason immediately asked.

"The young man in question was formerly a novice who joined the Vespertine Order at St. Kasimir's four years ago, to test his vocation. He informed me that the novices had to wait at table when the priory held important gatherings."

"So he incidentally overheard snatches of conversation?" his visitor surmised.

"Precisely," Lutz replied. "He told me - and I must admit to being skeptical about it at first - that the charter and insignia of the Potenti are housed at St. Kasimir's, and that secret initiation rites take place there periodically. What you have just related about the coat of arms displayed there would seem to support his account."

A slow smile of understanding dawned across his

visitor's intelligent features.

"Anything else," he enquired, "while we are on the subject?"

"He said that the hallmark of the society is mutual loyalty and absolute secrecy, something similar to the *Omerta* of the Sicilian mafia."

"That is extremely interesting, Herr Lutz," George Mason remarked, aware that he had found a very useful contact in the antiquarian. "It is also very valuable information. I am assuredly in your debt."

"In that case, would you wish to purchase the Thomas Mann?" Lutz quickly responded, with an eye to business.

"Absolutely," Mason said, reaching for his wallet as the bookseller carefully wrapped the reprint edition of *The Magic Mountain*.

"If I can assist you in any other way," Dieter Lutz said, "do not hesitate to contact me."

"That is most helpful of you," Mason said, pausing by the exit. "There is, as a matter of fact, something else you could perhaps look into while I am absent from Zurich."

"Gladly," the other replied, "if I am able to do so."

"Leonard Parks, when using the monogram F.M.P. on his computer files, appended the Latin words *Semper Diligens*. A fair English equivalent would be 'Ever Watchful'. You might try to find out for me, from your wife's relative, the former novice, what significance those words may have."

"I shall certainly do my best," the other assured him.

"I shall give you a call from my hotel as soon as I reach Zell tomorrow evening," his visitor added.

"That is a very beautiful area you will be traveling to, Herr Mason," the other said, with a touch of envy. "Some people rate the Austrian Tyrol even more highly than the

Swiss alps for scenic beauty. But I am not one of them."

CHAPTER SIX

Aristide Lebrun turned into a side-street off the Rue des Orfevres, a stone's throw from the Cathédrale de Notre Dame, and entered through the revolving door of a private hotel. He appeared more than usually preoccupied as he took the elevator to the second-floor conference room already occupied by a handful of his associates, who had been summoned there at his urgent request. He took his place at the head of the highly-polished table and did a quick mental check of those present, dispensing with the customary Gallic greeting of a kiss on each cheek.

"*Messieurs et Madame,*" he began, "please excuse me for the short notice I gave you to convene this meeting."

"Judging from your tone of voice on the telephone last evening," Jules Aubin, a marketing executive, said, "would I be correct in saying that we have problems?"

"Worse than you can possibly imagine," an ashen-faced Lebrun replied.

"We have been betrayed?" a third party, the industrialist Charles Gramont posited, with evident concern.

Aristide Lebrun shook his head and ventured a thin smile.

"Not quite as dire as that," he said, "but bad enough in its way."

"Does it concern the health of our Convenor, the Comte de Plesignac?" Jules Aubin enquired.

"The count, to my knowledge, remains in robust health, despite his eighty-odd years," Lebrun replied. "And, at all costs, he must receive no inkling of today's session. Nor must the other branches of our society. Is that clearly understood?"

The elite assembly muttered their agreement, focusing attention even more keenly on the speaker, waiting for him to elaborate.

Aristide Lebrun cleared his throat, served himself a glass of Vichy water from the table dispenser and said:

"As treasurer of the French Chapter, I very much regret having to make this announcement. As of this morning, *mes amis,* we are out of funds."

"Completely?" Charles Gramont enquired, in disbelief.

Lebrun gravely nodded.

"That cannot possibly be the case," Jules Aubin objected. "At out last meeting in March, you reported that we were in credit to the tune of a quarter of a million euros."

The treasurer raised his hands in a gesture of despair.

"Would that were the case today!" he exclaimed.

"How could such a large sum possibly go missing?" the industrialist pointedly asked, "unless someone embezzled it? You are the only person within our society, apart from the Convenor himself, who has the authority to sign checks."

"You surely recall, Charles," Lebrun defensively explained, "that it was your good self who recommended the services of Alphonse Benoit, the investment banker who specializes in off-shore accounts and similar tax-friendly schemes?"

"I did indeed," the industrialist vehemently replied. "He

has an excellent reputation in financial circles. Some of the wealthiest individuals in America and Europe, including scions of the old aristocratic families, avail themselves of his services. They have done for years."

The treasurer returned a look of irony, tinged with regret.

"Benoit is a crook," he bluntly announced. "He was arrested yesterday morning in Monaco and will be indicted before a French court here in Paris early next week. The news has not yet broken in the national press."

"Then how did you learn of it?" a skeptical Charles Gramont challenged.

"From a confidential source in the Fraud Squad," Lebrun replied. "Alphonse Benoit has over a period of years been operating what is known as a Ponzi scheme, so-named for the Italian swindler who devised it, while working at Boston in the 1920s."

"What exactly is a Ponzi scheme, Aristide?" Jules Aubin enquired.

"It is a very insidious form of fraud," the treasurer explained, as those in the know nodded agreement. "One that is extremely difficult to detect. The operator pretends to invest the monies entrusted to him. He pays all claims and dividends due to existing clients with money coming in from newer ones. Benoit's scheme only came unstuck after the severe downturn in global stock markets. New investment virtually dried up and his scheme was exposed, because he had insufficient funds to meet claims."

"That is outrageous," Celine Kervella, the fourth member of the small group, said. She was a woman of mature years who owned a perfumery in Provence. "Such schemes are old as the hills. Even Charles Dickens included one in his novel *Little Dorrit.*"

"How interesting, Celine," Jules Aubin remarked. "It

sounds typically Anglo-Saxon."

"There are many other victims, besides ourselves," Lebrun remarked, in self-defense. "All the paperwork seemed perfectly legitimate and, in more normal circumstances, Benoit's scheme could have continued for years without detection. Even the auditors were fooled by it."

There was a stunned silence lasting several minutes, as the implications of his revelation sank in.

"How do you propose to make up the loss?" Jules Aubin testily enquired.

"Unfortunately," the treasurer replied, "all normal channels of finance, in the way of donations, legacies and members' dues, have been fully tapped. We shall have to resort to extraordinary means."

"By which, presumably," Charles Gramont acidly remarked, "you mean extra-legal measures?"

"What other option is there?" a rather flustered Lebrun countered. "The funds have to be in place for our international convention, chaired by Sir Maurice Weeks. He is expecting us to offer a sweetener in the appropriate quarter, to secure the nomination of Colm Byrne as the next Finance Commissioner at Brussels. Once we control the key departments of the Commission, and especially the purse, we can tighten our grip on the European agenda and effectively side-line the European Parliament."

"So that our objectives," Jules Aubin said, "will not be subject to the whims of the electorate and their representatives at Strasbourg?"

"Precisely," Aristide Lebrun remarked. "As things stand at the present, all main initiatives already come from Brussels. Our objective will be to strengthen the bureaucracy and tighten our grip on it."

A pause ensued as the implications of his remarks sank in. Glasses were replenished with chilled Vichy water.

"Have you any comment," Celine Kervella then asked, "on what form the special measures you are anticipating might take? And please bear in mind, Aristide, that our credibility and standing vis-à-vis the other chapters in our society, particularly the German and the Finnish, will be seriously damaged if it should leak out that we have either lost money through ill-advised investment, or made up the deficit by questionable means."

All eyes focused on the treasurer.

"Leave the matter in my hands for the time being, *mes amis*," Aristide Lebrun said. "I shall come up with something, from my close contacts in financial circles. I shall arrange it so that any measures I feel it necessary to take shall not happen on our own doorstep. No one will be able to trace anything back to Paris."

"You are asking us for a great deal of trust, Aristide," Charles Gramont blandly remarked.

"And confidence," Jules Aubin pointedly added. "Which I sincerely hope will not be misplaced."

"Leave the matter with me, *Messieurs et Madame*," Aristide Lebrun said, considerably more relaxed now that he had broken the disastrous news and the inner circle of the French Chapter had grudgingly accepted the notion that all means possible must be considered to recoup their losses. The future of their society and its objectives depended on it. Rising to his feet, he said:

"I must now bid you all adieu. Time permitting, I should very much have liked to join you for lunch, in view of today's special offering from the chef, which I believe is to be ragout provençal. But I am afraid that will not be possible owing to a prior commitment. Until we meet again with more positive and encouraging news, *au revoir* and *bon appetit*."

So saying, he exited the room with a flourish, while his still shell-shocked associates slowly rose to their feet and transferred to the hotel restaurant, noted for its Mediterranean cuisine.

"A Ponzi scheme, would you believe it!" Celine Kervella scornfully remarked to Jules Aubin, as they entered the elevator.

*

The following morning, Sergeant Aubrey, after joining Inspector Mason for an early breakfast, went up to her room to pack her valise, leaving her colleague to linger in the restaurant over the morning paper. She was impressed that he could make some sense of the articles in the local broadsheet, *Tages Anzeiger*, resolving on her return to England to enquire about evening courses in foreign languages. She would like to build on her high school French as a way of increasing her availability for European assignments. Her task soon completed, she placed a call on her room telephone to Superintendent James Maitland at Scotland Yard.

"Maitland," came the curt response, as the line became live.

"Good morning, Superintendent," the detective sergeant said. "Alison Aubrey, calling from Zurich."

"Alison!" Maitland exclaimed. "Good to hear from you at last. How are things progressing?"

"Fine, so far," she replied. "We have just finished breakfast at Hotel Adler and shall be leaving shortly for Zell, in the Austrian Tyrol. Via Innsbruck."

"And how is Inspector Mason getting along with his enquiries?"

"It has been a most interesting and rewarding few days so far," the young officer confidently replied.

"Any sign of Leonard Parks?" the superintendent was keen to learn.

"None whatsoever, at this stage," Alison replied. "But we did manage to locate his mother, Léni Farkas, a frail elderly woman living in an industrial suburb of Zurich. She mentioned, among other things, that her son had paid her a visit during his stay here, about two weeks ago."

"Sounds quite promising, Alison," Maitland remarked. "And what did you glean from her, if anything?"

"She went on at some length about a priory at Glarus that her husband, Count Laszlo Farkas, had close connections with. She also told us that Leonard Parks, né Farkas, intended to visit his father's grave. So we made a detour to Glarus, to see if we could pick up the trail there."

There was a significant pause at the London end of the line.

"And what conclusions, if any, did you both draw from your visit to the priory?" Maitland eventually asked.

"Inspector Mason seemed to think there were some sort of curious goings-on at St. Kasimir's Priory, which is situated on a hillside overlooking the Wallensee."

"What gave him that idea, Alison?"

"We called for lunch at an inn in the town. Have you ever tried raclettes, Superintendent?"

"Never mind what you ate for lunch," the other testily replied. "Please answer my question."

"The innkeeper mentioned regular gatherings of prominent people," the chastened detective sergeant replied. "But he had no idea what it was all about. All very hush-hush, apparently. He said they sometimes used his inn for overflow accommodation from the priory guesthouse, and for evening get-togethers round the bar."

"Did Inspector Mason actually gain admission to St. Kasimir's?" Maitland immediately asked.

"Indeed he did," Alison replied. "But since women are not admitted, I visited the adjoining graveyard instead and sought out the count's burial plot. There were fresh flowers on it barely starting to wilt, indicating that they had been placed there quite recently."

She thought of also mentioning the German officers' plots she had noticed, but decided not to.

"The flowers were most likely from Leonard Parks," the superintendent remarked, "if his mother's account is reliable. But there the trail goes cold?"

"Not entirely," the young sergeant replied. "Parks, in the course of his tax investigations, interviewed an antiquarian bookseller here named Dieter Lutz. Lutz informed George Mason that his meeting with Leonard Parks had ended with a friendly compromise regarding his tax liabilities. Parks then apparently asked Lutz for travel directions to Zell."

"So you are off this very morning to the Tyrol," Maitland said, with a tinge of envy, "on the assumption that Mr. Parks met with no misadventure while visiting Zurich?"

"We are due to take the mid-morning train, to arrive there by early evening. Inspector Mason has made the necessary arrangements. I have just now finished packing my things, so I took the opportunity to call you from my hotel room."

"Good thinking, Alison," came the reply. "Have you any comments on Inspector Mason's performance generally?"

Alison Aubrey was a bit taken aback by that question.

Was she, a much less-experienced officer, being asked to pass judgment on the likes of George Mason? What exactly was the superintendent's game, she wondered?

"He comes across as very competent and professional," she tactfully replied. "He is also very good company and knows his way around."

"So you are enjoying your assignment?" Maitland said.

"Absolutely," Alison affirmed. "And it will be extra experience in Europe, for which I have you to thank."

"Do not mention it," the other affably replied. "Just keep me abreast of all major developments."

"I shall do my level best," she assured him.

That said, she replaced the receiver, zipped her valise and hauled it with some difficulty to the elevator, meeting George Mason in the foyer. He took over from there, leading the way along Limmatquai towards the Hauptbahnhof, where they bought tickets for the *Wiener Waltzer*, the crack mainline express to Vienna originating at Basel. Within minutes of their settling into the comfortable upholstery, the train eased slowly out of the station, skirting the high-rise tenements in the less affluent parts of the city.

"We made it in the nick of time," the detective said. "Have trouble packing?"

It was a veiled reference to the amount of time she had spent in her room after breakfast, but she could hardly explain that she had been on the telephone to London. He would be curious to know the reason why.

"Sorry I took so long," she apologized. "You know how it is, trying to find room for everything at the last minute."

George Mason smiled understandingly. His wife Adele, in similar circumstances, was prone to be dilatory.

"I took another look at Leonard Parks' diary before

retiring last night," he said. "Especially the telephone numbers."

"Really?" Alison enquired. "Anything of interest?"

He fished for the same in his jacket pocket and passed it across to her, pointing to one entry in particular.

"Felix Gertweiler," she read aloud, with a puzzled look. "Does that mean something to you, George?"

"Not as yet," Mason replied. "But it may soon do so. Apparently, the telephone entry for him is an Innsbruck number. I checked the dialing codes in the phone-book in my room. Just a short while ago, after you had gone upstairs to pack, I decided to ring the number from the hotel foyer."

"With what result?" she eagerly enquired.

"Gertweiler turns out to be a prominent philatelist in Innsbruck. His assistant, a young woman, gave me directions to his premises, which are handily quite near the main station. Since we change trains there while the *Wiener Walzer* continues on to Vienna, I thought I might just have time to pay him a visit."

"Just in case Leonard Parks called there?" she said, with a knowing smile.

"Let us for the moment say that it will help fill out our mental picture of the tax investigator and see what transpires. There must be a good reason for the number to be in the diary."

They lapsed into silence for a while, Alison taking in the scenery as the train eventually sped past a series of jagged peaks in the eastern alps known as the Churfuersten, the fabled Counts of Chur, which also lent its name to the Kurfuerstendamm in Berlin. George Mason engrossed himself in the copy of *The Times* he had obtained at the Zurich kiosk, mainly to check his small portfolio of stocks and catch up on the latest cricket scores. His home team, Yorkshire, he was pleased to note, stood at the head of the championship table. A brief stop at Buchs heralded the western end of the Arlberg Pass linking Switzerland with Austria. After another three hours of spectacular alpine views, the *Wiener Walzer* pulled slowly into Innsbruck, where they would transfer to the local service to Salzburg, which called at Zell.

"You relax awhile in the restaurant," Mason said, as they reached the station concourse, "and keep an eye on our luggage, while I seek out the philatelist. Our train leaves in just over an hour, so I shall be as quick as I can. Grab some refreshment, if you are peckish, while you have the chance."

Alison Aubrey made to do as instructed, feeling a little peeved at not being able to venture into this attractive university city on the River Inn. But George Mason was right. Somebody had to mind the luggage and she was, in fact, quite hungry after sitting four hours in the train with just a bottle of Perrier water for refreshment, so absorbed had she been with the alpine scenery to think of ordering a snack from the trolley. She waited until he had traded his Swiss francs for euros at the foreign exchange counter, so that she would have money to spend at the buffet, and watched him disappear into the busy street outside.

George Mason, following the directions given him by telephone that morning, proceeded along Maximilianstrasse as far as the intersection with Muellergasse. Taking a left turn, he soon came across a large, double-fronted shop with philately displays in both windows. He paused for a moment to admire them, wondering why he had never taken up stamp-collecting as a hobby, fascinating as it had always seemed to him. He noted with special interest a commemorative issue for the Commonwealth Games bearing a portrait of the Queen, before entering the premises. A plainly-dressed sales assistant with short brown hair and minimal make-up, whom he took to be his telephone contact, greeted him cordially.

"If possible, I should like to speak with Herr Gertweiler," he said.

"You must be the very person who rang this morning," the young woman replied. "I shall see if the proprietor is free."

The detective stood waiting as she went to the rear of the premises, casting his eye meanwhile over the displays beneath the glass top of the counter. They were mainly sets featuring Schubert, Mozart and Gustav Mahler, among others. Practically the whole gamut of Austrian composers. Within a few moments, a tall, elderly gentleman with thinning white hair and rimless spectacles emerged from the stockroom ahead of his young assistant, who immediately resumed her position behind the counter.

"You wished to speak with me?" the philatelist said, eyeing his visitor quizzically.

"I am trying to trace an acquaintance of mine, a Mr. Leonard Parks," Mason explained. "He may have called here in recent weeks."

"Herr Parks, of course," Gertweiler said. "He was here about - let me think, now – about two weeks ago."

"Did you meet him personally?" the detective asked.

"Indeed I did," came the reply. "At one time, before he moved to England, he was one of our regular customers. He dropped by quite recently on his way to Zell, to add some items to his collection."

"He was a serious philatelist then?" the detective asked.

"Of particular interest to him," the proprietor explained,

"were postage stamps minted during The Third Reich, to complete his set of military issues honoring the various branches of the armed forces. He also bought some rarer items, including one marking the first anniversary of the death of Reinhard Heydrich in 1942."

"Wasn't he the Gestapo official assassinated by Czech partisans at Prague?"

"Indeed he was," the other said, impressed at his visitor's knowledge of history. "The Nazis exacted a terrible reprisal for it on the citizens of Lidice, a small village in Bohemia."

"I think I have read somewhere about that," George Mason grimly remarked.

"Herr Parks also purchased a special edition commemorating the Anschluss," the philatelist recalled. "The annexation of Austria by Germany in 1938."

That particular tidbit, linked with the burial of Count Laszlo Farkas among graves of German officers at St. Kasimir's, caused the visitor to wonder if there had not been some close link between the Potenti, of which both Count Laszlo and his son appeared to be members, and The Third Reich. Although the Reich was long defunct, such a connection could indicate that the Potenti was a secret society with leanings to the far right. And if they were as powerful behind the scenes as Dieter Lutz had implied, what were the implications?

"Are you a collector yourself?" Gertweiler asked. "We have interesting new stock for the autumn season, when the faculty and student body return to the university."

"Afraid not," Mason admitted. "All I ever collected, and that rather haphazardly, is cricket memorabilia. But I am grateful for your information. You have been most helpful."

"Do not mention it," the other said, as the detective

moved towards the door. "Enjoy your visit to our country."

George Mason thanked him again and hurriedly retraced his steps down Maximilianstrasse, to catch up with Alison Aubrey, whom he found comfortably ensconced at a corner table in the first-class restaurant, just finishing a mushroom omelet. He sat down momentarily beside her.

"You haven't had any lunch, George," she remarked, with concern.

"I'll grab a sandwich from the deli and eat it in the train," he said. "Soon as you've done, we must transfer to Platform 8. Our connection to Zell leaves in just ten minutes."

Alison quickly finished her snack, rose from her place and accompanied her colleague across the main concourse, pausing momentarily while he purchased a ham and salad roll. Minutes later, they were settling into their seats in the train to Zell.

"How did you fare at Gertweiler's?" she enquired.

"I discovered, as I thought may have been the case, that our friend Leonard Parks called there on his way to Zell. He is, in fact, quite well-known to the proprietor."

"So he is a serious collector?"

"With a special interest in The Third Reich, apparently," Mason remarked.

"Which tells you what?" his intrigued colleague asked.

"At a shrewd guess," Mason said, "this Potenti outfit has strong right-wing leanings. Dieter Lutz thinks they are secretly aiming at world domination. But I think their ambitions may be more limited."

"What makes you say that?" Alison asked.

"The innkeeper at Glarus, if you recall, mentioned only Europeans gathering at the priory. If there had also been Americans, Africans or Asians present, they would have stood out, and he would have remarked on the fact. I would say that the Potenti's aims are focused mainly on Europe. "

"That is a logical inference, George," Alison conceded. "And you are beginning to think that Leonard Parks' fate, whatever that is, is somehow tied up with the Potenti?"

"I am certainly tending towards that view, Alison," he replied. "But let us see where the evidence leads. What we have so far is some rather interesting coincidences. And since Felix Gertweiler confirmed that Parks was going on to Zell, after calling at Innsbruck, we can safely assume we are on the right track."

"So far, so good," Alison encouragingly rejoined.

"Let us hope our luck holds," Mason pointedly remarked. "At least, we have the satisfaction of knowing that Parks reached Innsbruck in one piece."

The train was now some distance south of that city, entering rolling countryside dotted with picturesque small towns and villages, where the neat rows of dwellings displaying colorful window boxes captivated the young sergeant. After another hour, the mountains loomed ever larger until, as they entered Zell, they completely dominated the scenery on all sides. The lake the town was situated by was relatively small by alpine standards, but crystal-clear with a greenish hue from the reflections of dense stands of firs on either bank, the tree-line extending half-way up the mountainside. Remaining on the platform for a while to take in the view, they had the sensation of having entered another world, far from the traffic and hubbub of either Zurich or Innsbruck.

On leaving the station, they found themselves in the center of a small town of half-timbered buildings with flower-bedecked balconies, clustered round a compact square dominated by a Baroque church. They did not venture very far beyond the square before they came to a modest family hotel, Die Forelle Blaue which, now that the tourist season had passed its peak, offered a choice of rooms. The Scotland Yard agents checked in, deposited their luggage and freshened up before meeting again later in the foyer, where they studied a map of Zell showing the location of its key amenities, including the hospital, police station, tourist office, churches, hotels and recreational facilities. The university, they discovered, was located about a mile from the town center, on the north shore of the lake. It was too late in the day, George Mason considered, to pay it a visit and request a meeting with Professor Paul Jarvis, the third name on the tax investigator's list of people to be interviewed. Their priority for the moment was to relax after the long rail trek, sample the local cuisine at one of the inviting restaurants and get a good night's rest.

*

Alena Hruska felt flattered that Professor Jarvis should accord her an extra tutorial in his private chambers, to discuss in greater detail her essay on the Victorian poet Gerard Manley Hopkins, famous for a style known as sprung rhythm. A tall young woman, with strawberry-blond hair falling freely down her back, she paid scant attention to the oddly-matched couple who emerged from Die Forelle Blaue, just as she was passing the front entrance. A sophomore in the English Department, following a program in medieval and modern literature, she had opted to rent an apartment near the center of Zell, rather than share a room with another student at a hall of residence. She enjoyed the greater freedom and independence it offered, secure in the knowledge that her parents could well afford to indulge their only daughter. It was with a light step that she strode past the small hotel, glancing back momentarily as she caught the sound of English voices, thinking it was getting late in the season for tourists.

Her route in the encroaching dusk clung closely to the shore of the lake. It was deserted at this hour, most people being at dinner. But it was a route she had often taken alone at night, especially when returning to her apartment from an evening lecture in the university auditorium, so she had few misgivings. Not until, that is, a dark-colored sedan pulled up alongside and two men leapt out, confronting her. Despite her struggles and screams into the empty night, they succeeded in bundling her into the rear seat and drove off at high speed. Taking a right turn off the shore road, they headed into the foothills of the Kitzsteinhorn, coming to a halt an hour later outside a large wooden chalet of the type often rented to skiers. Without a word being said, she was led up the narrow outside staircase, through the sliding doors and into a sparsely-furnished bed sitting-room at the rear of the building. Her abductors secured the exits and promptly left.

Still in a state of panic, she switched on the table lamp and went directly to the window. It overlooked a steep ravine with dense tree-growth, providing no avenue of escape. Realizing that she was trapped, she slumped down on the bed, stared hard at the polished parquet floor and took stock of her situation. Through the inner door, she heard subdued voices speaking hurriedly in what sounded vaguely like the dialect of Carinthia. Her abductors, she decided, were Austrian. What could they possibly hope to gain by this stratagem, she wondered? And, more to the point, what would Professor Jarvis make of her failure to appear for the tutorial? Searching frantically for her cellphone, she realized that she had left it in her apartment at Zell, not anticipating a need for it that evening. A glance at her wristwatch told her it was just turned seven o'clock. After a while, overcome with a sense of despair and defeatism, she stretched out on the bed and fell fast asleep.

Later that evening, Paul Jarvis placed a call to Paris, to the suburban home of Aristide Lebrun. The latter had been made aware in advance of an urgent communication from Austria and had skipped an official dinner for the purpose. His phone rang at 8.15 p.m., at which hour he was alone in his study.

"Lebrun," he curtly responded.

"*Bonsoir*, Aristide," Paul Jarvis said. "I trust that all is well with you?"

"Never better," the Frenchman replied. "But my wife Sylvie has already retired for the night, with recurring migraine."

"Sorry to hear about that," the academic said. "I hope she soon improves."

"She takes medication for it," Lebrun replied "and normally recovers after a good night's sleep. What news from your end?"

"The bird is in the bag," the other cryptically replied. "An approach has been made to Alena's father regarding the ransom."

"Tell me a bit more about him," the other urged.

"Jan Hruska is the majority shareholder in one of Bohemia's largest breweries," Jarvis explained. "His net worth is in the millions of euros. Alena is his only child."

"So we can count on him coming through?" Lebrun said, gratified that the financial problems of the French Chapter could soon be resolved.

"It may take a few days," the academic cautioned, "for him to raise such a large sum of money. Then we must transfer it to your numbered account at Zurich."

"Just make sure there is no paper trail the authorities can pick up on," the Frenchman emphasized. "We do not want any last-minute hitches. The slightest whiff of publicity will sink us all."

"Put your mind at rest, Aristide," the other said. "This is a foolproof operation, in the hands of one of the most professional organizations in Austria."

"I knew I could count on you, Paul," the Frenchman said, with relief. "I recall your goodwill towards our branch of the society when you were a visiting lecturer at the Sorbonne."

"Halcyon days, Aristide," Paul Jarvis said, with feeling. "Unfortunately, now long past."

"But you have made excellent progress in the meantime," Lebrun assured him, "both in your academic career and in the wider arena."

Paul Jarvis knew at once that his French counterpart, while careful to avoid direct mention of the society, was referring to his steady rise through the ranks of the Potenti, something he owed partly to the good offices and patronage of Lebrun himself. If it was now his turn to repay a favor, so be it. He would not be found wanting, even if the educator in him reacted against the kidnapping, even for a brief period, of one of his most promising students. Poor Alena, he thought, salving his conscience with the knowledge that he had given express instructions to her abductors that there was to be no rough stuff, and that her basic needs were to be met without quibble. Contact with her family, however, was strictly off limits.

"Let me know, Aristide," he said, in conclusion, "when

your Zurich account has been credited."

"I shall be more than pleased to do that," Lebrun assured him. "Thank you again, Paul, for your invaluable help. It is a lifeline to the French Chapter."

CHAPTER SEVEN

Superintendent James Maitland had weighty matters on his mind when he arrived at Scotland Yard the following morning, feigning not to hear Bill Harrington's customary greeting before entering his office and closing the door firmly behind him. Seating himself at his teak desk, he immediately placed a call to the Exchequer.

"Put me through to Sir Maurice Weeks," he asked the telephonist, rehearsing in his mind how he was going to break the news to the First Secretary. Alison Aubrey's call from Zurich two days ago had set him thinking, and this was the first opportunity he had had to contact the senior civil servant.

"Weeks," came a rather pompous voice over the line.

"Sir Maurice," Maitland began, "there have been some interesting developments regarding Leonard Parks."

"You mean Inspector Mason has managed to discover his whereabouts?" the civil servant enquired, much surprised.

"Nothing so conclusive as that," the C.I.D. official replied. "But you are not going to believe what he *has*, in fact, turned up."

"And what might that be, Jim?" Weeks duly enquired.

"Somehow or other, he succeeded in contacting Parks'

aged mother living in the Zurich suburb of Oerlikon. She mentioned to him her family's close connections with St. Kasimir's Priory. According to Detective Sergeant Aubrey, who is keeping me abreast of developments by telephone, she and Mason visited Glarus a few days ago and began asking questions of local residents!"

"He cannot have discovered much," the civil servant evenly replied. "The prior, Father Dominic, is very close-mouthed, even for someone of his reclusive calling. And the local Swiss have no idea at all about what we discuss at our meetings. I would not lose any sleep over the matter, Jim, if I were you."

"But George Mason now knows that there are bi-annual gatherings of prominent people at the priory. Mason is a shrewd operator and may soon start putting two and two together."

"And making five," Maurice Weeks said, dismissively. "To get any handle at all on the deliberations and activities of the society, he would need in the first place to locate our website on the Internet. To access it, he would need to know our password. He may well form some vague notion of what takes place at Glarus, but similar top-flight gatherings of world leaders are held annually at St. Moritz and Davos, not to mention the deliberations of the United Nations in Geneva. To an outsider like George Mason, it will seem like just another top-level international gathering. Switzerland is, after all, the country most associated with such events."

"I expect you are right, Sir Maurice," James Maitland reluctantly conceded.

"Of course I am," the civil servant confidently asserted. "Ring me when you have some more significant developments to report. I am up to my ears in work here at the Exchequer. The prime minister and the chancellor want to start work on the new budget for the upcoming financial year."

Superintendent Maitland replaced the receiver with mixed feelings. Sir Maurice's sangfroid to some extent set his own mind at rest; yet not entirely. With anyone other than George Mason on the case, he too would have dismissed the Glarus episode as of minor importance. But the gritty Yorkshireman, he well knew, had a curious knack of ferreting things out, sometimes on the flimsiest of evidence. He consoled himself, however, as he turned his attention to more pressing police matters, particularly the recent spate of knifings on Wimbledon Common, that there was simply no way the inspector or any other outsider could access the society's website. Sir Maurice Weeks was certainly right about that. He also congratulated himself on assigning Alison Aubrey to the case. She owed him for that and could provide him with useful updates on the progress of her joint assignment with Mason.

*

The following morning, George Mason and Alison Aubrey reported for breakfast in the restaurant of Die Forelle Blaue, the latter noting with pleasure that the waitress was wearing traditional Tyrolean costume which complemented the rustic décor. Alpine motifs covered the walls, an alpine horn and a few primitive farm implements hung above a hearth stacked with logs for the approaching autumn season. Service was brisk, since only a handful of late tourists occupied the other tables. The detective was soon tucking into a mixed grill; while his colleague settled for muesli with yoghurt and fresh fruit, much enjoying the piped accordion music and the general ambience of the country hotel.

"Zell is such a lovely place," she remarked. "I could spend a vacation here."

"Why don't you?" George Mason replied. "Apart from the amenities Zell itself offers, there are several interesting trips on hand. You could take a cable-car up the Kitzsteinhorn, for example, for spectacular mountain views."

"Which one is the Kitzsteinhorn?" Alison asked.

"It is the tallest peak you can see when looking directly across the lake from the hotel entrance. You can't miss it. It is snow-capped year round."

"You have been reconnoitering, haven't you?" she teased, pouring cream into her freshly-brewed coffee.

"I woke early and took a stroll down by the lake," he admitted. "There is an elaborate chart on the strand that names all the local mountains, including the Pinzgau range to the north."

"And what else would you recommend, supposing I was to take a vacation here at some time in the future?"

"Berchtesgaden, Adolf Hitler's mountain retreat, is not all that far from here either. They apparently run bus trips to it from the railway station."

"I do not think I should want to go there," the young sergeant said, with a slight shudder. "Imagine making it a tourist attraction!"

"It is all a matter of history now," her colleague replied. "Moreover, they have converted the whole complex into a luxury hotel and sports center, I read somewhere."

"I suppose it might appeal to some," she grudgingly allowed, her attention distracted by the sparrows on the open window sill scavenging breadcrumbs.

"While you finish your coffee," the detective said, refolding his napkin and rising from the table, "I have a telephone call to make from my room. I shall meet you in about twenty minutes, outside the hotel."

"Where are we headed this morning?" she asked.

"To the university," he replied, thinking he would explain why later.

Back in his bedroom, he placed a call to Dieter Lutz, who was just opening up his bookstore at Schipfe.

"Good morning, Herr Mason," the antiquarian greeted. "How are things with you?"

"Can't complain," the detective replied. "I am calling from Zell, where we arrived yesterday evening."

"And how does it strike you, compared to Switzerland?"

"Similar, in many ways, but certainly more colorful. The dwellings are more brightly painted and the window boxes in full flower add a nice extra touch."

"Whereas here in Switzerland our domestic architecture is a little more somber," Lutz remarked. "It is the Calvinist influence, I expect."

"Both countries are very beautiful," Mason diplomatically replied, "in their own way. But I did not ring you to swap tourist impressions."

"Indeed not. When you left Zurich, you were keen to learn the significance of the words *Semper Diligens*," the antiquarian said. "And you are in luck, Herr Mason. My wife's relative, the young man I told you about who had entered the novitiate at St. Kasimir's, has approached an elderly friar, now retired, with whom he has remained in contact from time to time for spiritual counsel. Their close personal relationship permitted the friar to dispense, briefly, with the aura of secrecy surrounding events at the priory."

"He had no idea the enquiry came originally from Scotland Yard?"

"Certainly not," Lutz affirmed. "Otherwise, it would require *Omerta*, the vow of silence. The friar, Brother Fidelius, simply thought he was granting a small favor to the former novice, who had been under his tutelage during his time at St. Kasimir's."

"A lucky break for us, then," George Mason remarked. "So what is it all about?"

"*Semper Diligens*," the other explained, "could be rendered in English as 'Ever Watchful', or words to that effect."

"Dutifully sticking to one's appointed task?" the detective suggested.

"Exactly, Herr Mason. And in the overall configuration of the Illuminati, it is the motto of the lower order of members, known as the Diligenti, who occupy one rank below the Potenti They are not included in the inner, policy-making circles of the society, but they do nonetheless have a significant role to play. Particularly in areas such as fund-raising, routine administration and social functions."

"What sort of people are we now talking about?" a much intrigued George Mason asked him.

"Individuals, both men and women, from the middle orders of society," the bookseller explained. "They could be bank staffs, junior academics, administrators, civil servants, medical personnel. In fact, from almost any walk of life."

"Inland Revenue officials?" the detective immediately came back.

"Why not?" Dieter Lutz replied, with a knowing chuckle.

"I think I get the picture," Mason then said. "Leonard

Parks, in view of his middling social and professional status, could very possibly be a member of the Diligenti, rather than the Potenti. He recently visited St. Kasimir's Priory at Glarus and has since disappeared under the radar."

"That is something for you to look into," the bookseller rejoined. "I have done my small part, and I am counting on you, Herr Mason, to let none of this information get traced back to me. It could seriously compromise my sources, perhaps even affect my business. These are very powerful people you are looking into."

"You need have no fears on that score, Herr Lutz. Mum's the word," the detective assured him, before ringing off.

On his way down to the foyer, he weighed this interesting new development, but it did not seem at first glance to add very much to what he already suspected, that the tax investigator was indeed an active member of a secret society. Perhaps the significance of Lutz's disclosure about ranks within the Illuminati would become clearer in the days ahead, he mused, as he stepped outdoors to catch up with his colleague. Not spotting her immediately, he eventually found her among the stalls of a street market that had been erected on the far side of the main square.

"So here you are," he said. "I was wondering where you had got to."

"I cannot resist open-air markets," Alison replied, falling in step with him towards the lake shore. "Each one is quite unique, in the variety of wares it offers."

"Find anything of interest?" he casually asked.

"I was admiring items on the craft stalls, mainly wood carvings of local fauna like the chamois. I was almost tempted to buy one, but they are quite expensive."

"Aimed at the tourist trade, no doubt," Mason remarked.

They soon gained the footpath by the lake, heading in the direction of the university, pausing only to watch the ferry to Thumersbach depart from the jetty, sending the resident swans and ducks scuttling from its path. He pointed out the Kitzsteinhorn, whose snow-capped peak reflected in the clear waters of the Zellersee brought a gasp of wonderment from his young colleague. Within twenty minutes, they had reached the university campus, following behind small groups of students making their way from the halls of residence to the main building. On entering, the detectives approached the information desk.

"I wish to make an appointment with Professor Jarvis," Mason said.

"You name?" the receptionist enquired.

"George Mason, from London."

"I shall see if he is available," the woman replied, consulting the roster of lecturers for the morning session. She then picked up the house phone and placed a call.

The two visitors exchanged hopeful looks.

"Professor Jarvis will see you straight away," the officer said. "Go directly up to his study, Room 315."

"That is a stroke of luck," Mason remarked to his colleague, as they mingled with young people mounting the broad staircase to the second floor, which housed the English Department. They quickly found the academic's study.

"Enter," came a deep baritone from within, in reply to their tentative knock.

The two visitors stepped inside, to be confronted by a large gentleman over six feet tall, with short sandy hair, smoking a pipe of aromatic tobacco, which he immediately laid aside.

"From London, eh?" he said heartily, inviting them to sit.

"What brings you to our modest seat of learning?"

Alison Aubrey glanced towards her senior colleague.

"We are from Scotland Yard," George Mason said, producing ID as he gauged the effect of his words.

The academic's perceptible frown soon gave way to a quizzical smile.

"It is about income tax, isn't it?" he said, much like a schoolboy caught red-handed. "Mind you, I never imagined they would put the C.I.D. on my trail."

"In a manner of speaking, Professor Jarvis, that is correct," the detective replied. "I am aware, for example, that you maintain a bank account in the Cayman Islands, to shelter part of your earnings from the British tax authorities."

"A Mr. Leonard Parks, from the Inland Revenue, came to see me less than a month ago, about the very same thing," Paul Jarvis admitted.

"How did Mr. Parks strike you on that occasion?" Sergeant Aubrey asked. "I mean, did he seem worried, or preoccupied about something? Or would you say his manner was perfectly normal?"

The professor seemed a little taken aback at the unexpected line of questioning.

"Now let me think," he slowly answered, while opening the study window to clear the pipe smoke. "At the outset of the interview, his manner was much as I would have expected from a taxman."

"What manner would that be?" Alison asked.

"Well, to be perfectly honest," the other replied, "it was rather confrontational and challenging. He accused me of salting away royalties from my various publications in an off-shore account. He wanted me to make a clean breast of things and square my record with the British tax authorities."

"Publications?" Mason asked, for the first time noticing a small wooden shield on the cluttered desk, which was half-turned towards the window.

The professor rose and scanned his bookshelves, before taking down two large tomes. While he was so occupied, the detective craned his neck and stole a quick glance at the face of the shield, almost gasping aloud in surprise as he did so. Alison wondered what on earth he was doing and gave him a slightly reproving look. George Mason glanced impishly back at her, as Paul Jarvis turned and passed the two volumes across the desk.

"Standard textbooks in Modern English Literature," he announced, with evident pride. "I must admit they have earned me a deal of money, especially after the American edition came out last year. I do not see why the tax people should take a cut, but if they have gone to the extent of putting Scotland Yard on my trail, they must mean business."

The two visitors politely perused the blurb on the book covers and cursorily sampled the contents, before handing them back, Alison taking more time than her colleague. English Literature had been one of her favorite subjects at school, prompting her to read it at Sussex University, as part of her degree course. Paul Jarvis noted her interest with approval.

"We are not here regarding your tax affairs," George Mason explained. "We are much more interested in Leonard Parks. He has gone missing."

The academic's expression registered both relief and concern.

"What do you mean by missing?" he enquired. "Mr. Parks was here in this very room only a short while ago."

"In the meantime," the detective said, "he has gone completely under the radar. No word to his wife, to his mother in Zurich, or to his office at Manchester."

"I find that very difficult to believe," the academic remarked, apparently much concerned.

"You said his manner was much as you expected at the start of his interview," the detective then said. "Does that mean it altered during the course of your meeting?"

"Indeed, it did," came the reply. "As the discussion proceeded, he seemed to lose the thrust of his argument, as if his mind was on something else entirely."

"Have you any idea what it was that so preoccupied him?"

The professor shook his head regretfully.

"So how did what sounds like a rather unproductive interview conclude?" Mason asked.

"Mr. Parks simply said that he would be in touch with me again, but he did not say exactly when that might be."

"So you felt let off the hook?" Alison suggested.

"To some extent, yes," the other replied. "Mr. Parks gathered up his official papers and left rather hurriedly. He said he had a train to catch."

"Did he say where he was headed?" Mason asked.

"Budapest, if I remember correctly."

The two visitors exchanged puzzled glances, while Paul Jarvis returned his textbooks to the shelves. Regaining his seat, he took up his pipe again and pensively lit it, blowing a cloud of aromatic smoke towards the open window, in order not to discomfort his visitors.

"Tell me, Professor," George Mason pointedly asked, "had you ever met Leonard Parks before, apart from your recent interview about income tax?"

The academic reacted in some surprise.

"Absolutely not," he replied. "What prompted such a question?"

"Just a thought," his visitor said, "running through my mind."

"If I could offer you further assistance, I would," Jarvis then said. "But I am due in the lecture theatre in ten minutes, if you will excuse me. I need to collate my notes beforehand."

With that, he began assembling slips of paper lying across his desk.

"I do not think we need take up more of your time, Professor," George Mason said, taking the strong hint while rising to his feet. "Our visit here has already, in fact, proved quite useful in a certain way."

"Glad to hear it," the other said, showing them to the door in a more affable manner, now that questions of taxation had taken a back seat.

Once outside the building, the two detectives rethreaded their way through the campus and regained the footpath along the shore, pausing to watch a rowing team in training and the half-dozen sail boats on the open water. George Mason checked his watch. It was approaching noon, almost time for a spot of lunch. As they walked, he kept his eye open for a suitable venue, where they could take advantage of the fine weather to eat outdoors.

"What made you ask the professor if he had previously met Leonard Parks?" a puzzled Alison Aubrey asked, the moment they were seated outside a lakeside cafe near the center of Zell.

"It certainly has nothing to do with income tax," her colleague assured her, scanning the menu. "Care to share a pizza, with mixed salad?"

The young sergeant nodded in agreement. A light lunch

was all she could face after a late breakfast.

"You are evading my question, George," she said, as Mason's attention was distracted by the boating activity on the lake.

He turned his gaze back towards her, with a slow smile.

"Both Paul Jarvis and Leonard Parks are members of a secret society known as the Illuminati," he explained. "But I suspect they belong to different, and presumably watertight, branches."

"Like the secret service," Alison suggested, on sudden inspiration.

"How do you mean?" he queried.

"In the secret service, no one section knows what goes on in the others. It is the principle of fragmented knowledge. If a given agent is arrested, he cannot then spill the beans on other agents and jeopardize the entire organization, because he only understands his own limited role."

"Good thinking, Alison," George Mason responded. "The Illuminati may well operate on similar lines. For your information, it all hangs on the motto *Semper Diligens*, which appears in Leonard Parks' diary. I have it on good authority from my source in Zurich that those words signify a member of the Diligenti, who are a step lower in rank to the Potenti. Both ranks come under the Illuminati umbrella."

"Your source being the antiquarian bookseller at Schipfe?" Alison asked, delicately forking a portion of the ham-and-artichoke pizza.

The detective, amused that she had put two and two together regarding his private visits to Dieter Lutz, nodded agreement.

"I can appreciate how you tie Leonard Parks in with this

strange society," she continued. "But how on earth did you identify Professor Jarvis as a member, from the short visit we paid him?"

"You noticed, while we were in his study, that there was a miniature shield on his desk," Mason explained. "You in fact gave me a rather questioning glance when I took a peek at it as the professor turned away. It bears the self-same coat of arms as the shield mounted on the wall at St. Kasimir's Priory!"

"You don't say so, George!" an intrigued Alison Aubrey exclaimed. "Would that perhaps account for Leonard Parks' sudden change of demeanor part-way through his interview with the professor?"

"Quite possibly," her colleague agreed. "If Parks noticed that shield, and I can't see how he could have missed it, he would have realized that he was pursuing a senior member of the society for tax evasion. The ethic of the Illuminati is absolute and unquestioning loyalty, as well as *Omerta,* signifying complete silence and discretion, along the lines of the Italian mafia."

"That would have placed someone like Leonard Parks in a real bind," Alison surmised, sipping her spritzer. "A question of divided loyalties, in view of his dedicated service to his employer, the Inland Revenue."

"Which would explain," Mason agreed, "why, part-way through his interview with Jarvis, he began to soft-pedal. It would have gone completely against the grain to pursue the Revenue's case."

"You are quite a perceptive guy, George," she remarked. "No wonder you have such a formidable reputation."

George Mason, gratified to bathe in his young colleague's high regard, brushed the compliment aside.

"It is merely a question of logical inference," he said,

dismissively. "Any well-trained detective could do the same."

"I doubt it," Alison said, with conviction. "So far so good. In the light of what we have learned here in Zell, what is our next move?"

Mason quickly finished his half-pizza and endive salad and took a swig of his pilsner.

"Next objective, Budapest," he announced, "via Vienna. In a short while, we shall return to our hotel, check out and take the next train back to Innsbruck, where we catch up with our old friend, the *Wiener Waltzer*. It will speed us to the Austrian capital in double-quick time. We should be there by early evening."

"How exciting," his young colleague said, "to think that we shall soon be by the Danube. I can hardly wait."

CHAPTER EIGHT

The *Wiener Waltzer* pulled into Vienna Westbahnhof at 6.35 p.m. The two detectives, having broken their journey briefly at Salzburg to view Mozart's house, transferred to Hotel Graf, whose upper windows overlooked the extensive grounds of the Schoenbrunn Palace, the former residence of Austrian emperors. The Graf was a modest family hostelry that did not offer a full restaurant service. After checking in, they set off to explore their immediate environs, partly to walk off the effects of sitting several hours in the train, before settling down to a late meal at one of the city's celebrated coffee houses. Alison Aubrey was intrigued to discover that the Viennese used such places for all manner of agreeable activities: to play chess, write letters, read books, or simply to while away the time in conversation with friends. Its ambience was similar in some ways to London pub-restaurants of the more upmarket kind, such as one might find in Chelsea, Mayfair or Belgravia.

George Mason, having finished his meal and ordered coffee, was scanning a copy of the local evening newspaper, the *Wiener Abendblatt,* which he had bought at the station kiosk.

"Listen to this, Alison," he said, sitting bolt upright.

The young sergeant, who had been taking stock of the

establishment's varied clientele, while also following the moves in a nearby game of chess, looked expectantly towards him.

"You are not going to believe this," he continued. "A young student was recently kidnapped from Zell University."

"You don't say so, George!" Alison remarked. "Does it give details?"

"It says here that she is the daughter of a prominent Czech brewer, Jan Hruska. A millionaire, apparently. A large ransom has been demanded for her release. The police have been warned to keep their distance."

"I wonder if Professor Jarvis was aware of this when we spoke with him earlier?" Alison remarked.

"Well, if he wasn't then," Mason assured her, "he most certainly will be now. It'll be in all the media."

"Poor girl," Alison said, with feeling. "I sincerely hope she does not come to any harm."

"It seems an odd sort of place for a kidnapping," Mason said. "Zell struck me as such a quiet, peaceful town, where parents would reasonably expect their children to be completely safe."

"Is anywhere completely safe, these days?" his colleague sadly reflected.

Their meal finished, they walked slowly back to their hotel. When they reached it, Alison did not join George Mason for a nightcap in the bar. Feigning weariness, she went straight up to her room, took a warm shower and relaxed for a while on the comfortable divan, listening to music on the radio. A glance at the wall clock told her it was a little past ten o'clock. Time, she decided, to place a call to Superintendent Maitland, who had given her both his home and office number. Turning down the radio volume, she picked up the phone and requested an outside line. After misdialing a couple of times, she finally got through.

"Good to hear from you again, Alison," James Maitland said. "Where are you calling from this evening?"

"From Graf Hotel, Vienna," Alison replied. "And isn't this just the most wonderful city? The streets are so long and broad, it would take hours to get round just the main tourist sights."

"I can imagine," Maitland said, "since it was built on an imperial scale."

"We just got back from dinner," Alison then explained, "in a charming coffee house. I left George Mason in our hotel bar."

"Where I fully imagined he would be at this hour," the other rather caustically replied. "What progress so far, Alison?"

"We were in Zell earlier today, interviewing a Professor Paul Jarvis at the university there. He confirmed that Leonard Parks had visited him a few weeks ago regarding his tax affairs."

"But still no sign of Parks himself?" the superintendent was quick to ask.

"Parks informed Jarvis that he was on his way to Budapest," Alison explained. "We shall be heading there tomorrow."

"Is that all you have discovered, Alison?"

"Inspector Mason seems to think that both the professor and Leonard Parks are members of some sort of secret society," Alison added. "He is also beginning to suspect that may have some bearing on the taxman's present whereabouts."

There was a long pause at the London end of the line, making the caller wonder if she had said the wrong thing.

Eventually, James Maitland testily asked:

"How on earth does Inspector Mason arrive at such a conclusion?"

"Something to do with mottoes and a miniature coat of arms displayed on the professor's desk. George Mason noticed the same coat of arms at St. Kasimir's Priory and made a connection between them."

There was another pregnant pause.

"Very perceptive of him," Maitland reluctantly allowed.

"Keen as mustard, in fact," Alison said. "I feel sure he will get to the bottom of this business, given time."

"I do not doubt it," the superintendent replied, with feeling. "Thank you for your call this evening, Alison. Do not forget to ring when you reach Budapest, to keep me fully abreast of any new developments."

"I shall certainly do that, Superintendent," Alison Aubrey assured him, putting down the phone before slipping off her bathrobe and changing into her pajamas, anticipating a good night's sleep ahead of their trip across the border. As if to set the right mood for a visit to Hungary, a program of folk music came over the radio. Alison turned the volume back up and listened contentedly for a while, before calling it a day.

*

The next day, after a light buffet breakfast at the hotel, George Mason booked a taxi to take them through the busy center of the city as far as the Danube embankment. After proceeding for a while along a main artery named Lassallestrasse, it drew to a halt at the Handelskai, where the Scotland Yard pair alighted. Looming before them were the elegant lines of a large river-boat, the *Orsova*, with prospective passengers already mounting the gangway. Beyond that, the detective spotted the giant Ferris wheel he recalled seeing in the Orson Welles World War 11 movie, *The Third Man,* based on the novel by Graham Greene. There it loomed, plain as day, in the middle of the Prater, the large public space abutting the river. He then espied the booking office a short distance away and steered his young companion towards it, purchasing tickets for the overnight voyage to the Hungarian capital. That done, they mounted the gangway and sought out their cabins on B-deck. Half-an-hour later, Alison Aubrey caught up with her senior colleague in the forward bar, just as the *Orsova* was edging away from the quay.

"Isn't this something?" she remarked, sitting on the bar stool next to him. "I never imagined, when I left London, that I was in for a Danube cruise."

"I thought you might prefer it to the train," Mason said, rather pleased with himself for arranging it. "It costs a fair bit more, but our budget will stretch to it. What will you have to drink?"

"I shall settle for something rather light for the moment," she replied. "A spritzer, perhaps."

The detective ordered for her and suggested transferring to one of the tables on the foredeck, to give them a better view of the passing scenery.

"Cabin satisfactory?" he enquired.

"It is a little cramped," Alison said, "and it has a rather dank feel to it. You can almost smell the river."

"Because it is down on B-deck, near the water line," he explained. "The superior cabins on A-deck will be airier, but they are also quite a bit pricier. We shall have to make do with what we have."

"I think it is just terrific, George," his young colleague enthused. "I would not have missed it for anything."

In the course of that afternoon, the *Orsova* made steady progress through the deep countryside of southern Austria, past elegant villas and quaintly picturesque villages, before crossing the border into Slovakia. Around four o'clock, a large city loomed on the left-hand bank and a group of tourists gathered on the foredeck with their cameras. From what he could discern from their age and snippets of conversation, George Mason took them to be retirees from Switzerland. A younger woman, presumably their guide, gathered them together in a compact group and began to address them. The detective rose from his place and hovered on the periphery, hoping to pick up snatches of the guide's commentary as the ship cruised past broad landscaped gardens replete with picnicking family groups and casual strollers. A riverside walk and cycle track completed the amenities.

"Bratislava," he informed his companion, who had joined him at the ship's rail to take in the view.

"It looks like quite a large city," Alison remarked. "Attractive too. Full of open spaces."

"The largest riverside city in Slovakia," George Mason said, repeating what the guide had told her Swiss clientele.

The guide herself, having concluded her brief commentary, overheard English voices and turned towards them.

"It is not very often we meet British tourists on the Danube," she said, in competent English. "Germans, quite often. And Swiss, like my party from Basel. Very occasionally, we come across American tourists."

The detective was not about to disillusion her by

revealing the true purpose of his voyage. If she thought he and Alison were ordinary tourists, he saw no harm in that. And if she thought, as she evidently did, that despite their age difference they were a couple, there was no harm in that, either.

"A nice-looking city," he remarked.

"Bratislava is indeed quite lovely," the guide agreed. "Visegrad is another fine city on the border with Hungary. We shall sail past it during the night, so unfortunately you will miss it."

"What is so special about Visegrad?" a curious Alison Aubrey enquired.

"For one thing, it is strategically situated on a bend of the river," came the reply, "giving it good defenses during the many conflicts of bygone centuries. It is also rich in period architecture."

"From the classical era?" George Mason enquired, thinking of the Roman province of Transdanubia, which would have included this area.

The tour guide nodded.

"In the fourth century," she explained, "Emperor Constantine erected a fort there, the ruins of which are still extant. Centuries later, a Hungarian king named Matthias built a Renaissance palace on the hillside. One could spend a whole afternoon looking over it. Apart from the historic architecture, people visit Visegrad for the thermal springs, as a cure for rheumatism, gout and similar ailments."

"You and your party are traveling to Budapest?" Alison asked.

"Actually," the woman said, "we are continuing on to Belgrade, before returning by rail to Vienna. From there, we shall fly back to Basel at the conclusion of the trip."

"An interesting itinerary," George Mason remarked,

thanking her for the information and returning to his seat, while his more active colleague descended to the lower deck, to visit the boutiques. On her return, she quickly finished her drink and repaired to her cabin to rest awhile before dinner.

George Mason joined her later in the main restaurant, situated on the top deck to enhance the view. Wearing a print dress, Alison took her seat opposite him at a window table, as the remaining places filled up with members of the Swiss party led by the friendly guide, and assorted couples the detective thought might be German or Dutch. After a long interval, during which aperitifs were served, a waiter approached them with the menu. They studied it carefully.

"I think I shall settle for something rather light," Mason said. "River fish might be a good choice."

His companion, puckering her brow, took a while to decide. At length, she said:

"I am going to try one of the regional dishes, something that would be difficult to find a truly authentic version of back home. Probably the goulash."

"How about a glass of Egri Bikaver to help it down?"

"And what exactly would that be, George?" she cautiously enquired, aware of a certain mischievous streak in his character.

"It is a noted Hungarian red," Mason replied. "Bull's Blood, in plain English."

"I am game, if you are," she replied, rather warily. To her, it sounded like the sort of full-bodied vintage men would typically go for. A wine with macho overtones and a hint of bull-fighting.

As if reading her thoughts, he added:

"It is quite a mild wine, actually, Alison. Soft on the palate. I feel sure you will enjoy it."

The young sergeant smiled approvingly, pleased that he had her interests at heart. Having placed their order, they sat back to enjoy the scenery, as the *Orsova* headed at a good rate of knots towards the Hungarian border.

"I could take to a life like this," he remarked, the moment their food arrived. "I wonder if they hire detectives on these boats?"

"You are romancing, George," Alison teased. "For one thing, you would be giving up your benefits, including pension entitlement, if you left the police service. Let us be practical and concentrate on the business in hand. What exactly do you propose to do when we reach Budapest?"

"I have already given that some thought," he replied, forking what he took to be a local species of trout. "At least, initially. What happens after that is anyone's guess. How is the goulash, by the way?"

"Delicious," she said, "if a bit heavy on the paprika."

"When we reach Budapest," he continued, "I aim to make contact with a person named Milos. Justine Parks, Leonard's wife, claimed that he was an old college friend of her husband. I am hoping he may be able to throw some light on the taxman's whereabouts."

"How can we be sure that Parks reached Budapest?" she asked.

"We can't be, Alison," Mason remarked. "But, so far, he has put in an appearance at all points on his official itinerary. I should be very surprised if he has not turned up there, especially if he intended to meet with an old friend he had not seen in years."

"How will you be able to get in touch with this Milos?"

"His phone number is in Parks' diary," Mason told her, "handed to me at Hotel Adler in Zurich, courtesy of the manager. We shall try placing a call from a telephone kiosk soon after the *Orsova* docks tomorrow morning."

"Intriguing, isn't it, George," she said, quite enjoying the palatable wine, "not knowing what lies ahead?"

"You can say that again, Alison," her colleague remarked, with feeling. "The uncertainty adds to the appeal of the job, I grant you. But in this instance, I would settle for less uncertainty and more in the way of hard facts."

*

Aristide Lebrun arrived early that evening at London St. Pancras, having taken the late-afternoon Eurostar via the Channel Tunnel, a rail journey of just over two hours from Paris. He immediately took a cab to the Maida Vale home of Sir Maurice Weeks, who was expecting him. The butler answered the door and showed the Frenchman into the reception room of a large, stone-built mansion set in its own grounds in a leafy cul-de-sac. Within minutes, the senior civil servant appeared and bade good-bye to his wife, who was on her way to a West End theater, before joining his visitor, being careful to close the room door behind him. Butlers, in his long experience of them, were all ears.

"I gather you have some good news, Aristide," he began, keenly appraising the Frenchman, while inviting him to sit.

"The required funding is now in place," Lebrun explained. "Paul Jarvis has banked it in his personal account on the Cayman Islands."

"All legitimate contributions from reputable sources, I take it? Sir Maurice pointedly asked.

"*Absolument, Monsieur,*" his visitor replied, with as straight a face as he could muster.

"So we now have sufficient means to ensure nomination

of our own candidate for commissioner?" the Exchequer official asked.

"With the Finance Department in our grasp," Lebrun assured him, "we shall effectively control a key area of the European Commission."

"Which will enable you to fully implement the society's agenda," Sir Maurice said, with satisfaction. "And put an end, at least for the next several years, to the liberal and left-wing programs currently in vogue."

He rose from his chair and crossed the room to the cocktail cabinet, where he poured two large measures of cognac.

"Let us drink to that," he said, offering his visitor a glass.

Aristide Lebrun rose to his feet, standing several inches shorter than his host.

"*Faciant meliora potentes!*" he proposed, with a confident air.

"Let those who can do better," Sir Maurice echoed in English, resuming his seat. "And now that the Potenti shall soon hold the purse strings, there is no limit to what may be achieved. The clock can be turned back a generation, at least across the European Continent if not now here in Britain following Brexit, to get people working again the way they used to in the old days. Welfare benefits and similar disincentives to productive employment will be cut back."

"The International Labor Office may present some problems," the Frenchman cautioned.

"Then find a way round them," Weeks said. "I would be more concerned about the activities of a certain member of Scotland Yard Special Branch, than anything the I.L.O. can throw at you."

"What exactly do you mean by that, Sir Maurice?" his

concerned visitor asked.

"I am referring to a certain Inspector George Mason. He is currently on assignment in Europe trying to locate a tax investigator named Leonard Parks, who has apparently gone missing."

"What possible bearing could that have on the affairs of the Potenti?"

"From the fact that Leonard Parks is a member of our junior branch, the Diligenti," Sir Maurice explained. "Mason may possibly have apprised himself of the existence of our society and possibly also of Parks' membership in it. I have it on good authority that the detective recently visited St. Kasimir's Priory, for example."

"Could Mason also be aware of Paul Jarvis's role in the scheme of things?" Lebrun asked, nervously sipping his cognac.

"Not unless Jarvis himself informed him of the fact," came the reply. "Which I very much doubt. I am aware that they met recently, since the professor was on Leonard Parks' list of candidates to interview regarding tax evasion."

"How is it that you are aware of these matters?" an impressed Aristide Lebrun enquired.

"I have my contacts at Whitehall," the other replied. "And the Comptroller General of Revenues is a personal friend of mine. We play bridge together. I got it from him that Professor Jarvis often transferred royalties from his widely-used textbooks into the same off-shore account we are using for the Potenti's slush fund. Leonard Parks may have grown aware of that, in the course of their recent meeting."

"And that knowledge would have caused him an agony

of indecision," the Frenchman surmised. "It would be a question of proceeding with enquiries that may have led to a court case involving one of our key members, or..."

"...of backing off completely," the civil servant added, "thus reneging on his official duties as an agent of the Inland Revenue."

Aristide Lebrun put down his glass, rose from his chair and paced the room, absorbing the full implications of this new turn of events.

"But even supposing this Inspector Mason may somehow have grown aware of our society," he eventually said, "he cannot possibly move forward on that knowledge and unmask our objectives, without accessing our website. I very much doubt he understands Latin, for one thing."

"Recruits to the police service in Mason's day came directly from high school," Sir Maurice Weeks explained. "Only quite recently have they begun to accept graduates in criminology, much to the disgust of Superintendent Maitland. He regards such recruits as too ivory tower, ill-suited to the nitty-gritty of routine police work."

"So we can confidently assume that Mason knows no Latin?" his visitor asked.

"It was dropped years ago from British school curricula," the other explained. "And I doubt that George Mason, adept as he apparently is at French and German, according to Chief Inspector Bill Harrington, would have taken pains to learn a dead language. It does, however, still have its supporters. There is a daily radio broadcast in Latin from Helsinki, of all places. *Nuntii Latini*, I believe it is called. One of my colleagues at the Exchequer regularly tunes into it."

"The Finns are about the last people I would associate with the Latin language," Lebrun wryly observed, setting down his empty glass. "But all power to them. More to the point, Sir Maurice, is that George Mason would need to know our Latin password, in order to access our website."

"I doubt he is well-versed in classical sources," his host drily observed, laying aside his glass in turn and rising to his feet. "Now, if you would care to join me for dinner, Aristide? I expect you may have quite an appetite after your trip from Paris."

"That is most thoughtful of you, Sir Maurice," the Frenchman said, following his host into the dining-room. "I should be delighted to accept your legendary hospitality."

"It is the least I can do, *mon cher ami*, in the circumstances, and in view of your dedicated service to our society," the civil servant said. "Sorry my wife Hermione could not join us on this occasion. She booked a theater trip to the West End with her sister and brother-in-law some weeks ago. One of those modern, experimental plays. I have little time for them myself. Give me Shakespeare or Ibsen any day."

"You would also enjoy Molière," his guest said, keen to promote his native culture.

"They sometimes present his plays at the Institut Francais, Queensbury Place," Sir Maurice replied. "In fact, I fully intend to accompany Hermione to the upcoming performance of *The Hypochondriac*. One day next month, I believe."

"An excellent choice," Aristide Lebrun remarked. "*Le Malade Imaginaire* is one of my favorite pieces of theatre."

"They also promote classic French films, such as *Jules et Jim.*"

"All the more reason to go," the other replied.

CHAPTER NINE

Around mid-morning of the following day, the skyline of the Hungarian capital loomed ahead. Most of the passengers aboard the *Orsova* gathered on the foredeck with their cameras, while the two detectives lingered over breakfast in the restaurant. Emerging into the open air thirty minutes later, they soon appreciated the tourists' motivation. The river approach presented a most arresting sight. The Danube cut right through the heart of the city, separating Buda on the left bank from Pest on the right. The friendly Swiss guide pointed out the Fisherman's Bastion, the neo-Romanesque structure built along the base of Castle Hill in Buda as a defense against marauding Turks in the sixteenth century. Pest, she informed them, had originally been a separate city that now housed the Hungarian Parliament and other official buildings. At its center was the Belvaros, an enclave of narrow streets and compact squares dating from the Middle Ages.

When the boat finally docked on the Pest side of the river soon after eleven o'clock, Inspector Mason and Sergeant Aubrey disembarked ahead of the Swiss tour party and made their way in bright sunshine from Elizabeth Quay to Andrassy Street, where they checked into a modest hotel before setting out to acquaint themselves with their new environment. After proceeding a short way down the main boulevard, past elegant shopping malls that spoke of post-Communist prosperity, they were soon drawn into the old-world ambience of the Belvaros, fascinated by the variety of its boutiques, stores and restaurants. After a while, they paused for cool drinks at Café Vlad, one of the small establishments that typically lined the crowded sidewalks. Mason asked to use the telephone, dialing the number for Milos Foldes listed in Leonard Parks' diary. Within minutes he returned to his seat, with a disappointed look.

"Something wrong, George?" Alison immediately asked.

"There was no reply," the detective said. "Most likely, he will be at work. I shall try again later."

"We have the whole afternoon ahead of us," Alison said. "We should try to escape the heat. It must be in the high eighties."

Mason consulted his guidebook, while sipping his chilled lemon juice.

"We could visit one of the art museums," he suggested. "There are quite a number that look interesting."

"For example?" his companion asked.

"There's the Museum of Contemporary Art, for instance, exhibiting paintings and sculptures from the last half-century."

"The term contemporary art can cover almost anything nowadays," Alison wryly commented. "I would prefer something more traditional."

"Then how about the National Gallery?" he colleague replied. "It is not very far from here, according to my street map. It houses Hungarian art from the Middle Ages down to modern times, including wood sculpture, religious artifacts, Renaissance and Baroque paintings."

"That sounds more my cup of tea," Alison replied. "And

it will give us the opportunity to learn something of the history and culture of this fascinating country, which also happens to be Leonard Parks' country of birth."

"It should help fill out our mental picture of him," Mason agreed.

The young sergeant sipped her iced drink thoughtfully for a while, seemingly observing the motley crowd strolling past the café, before saying:

"Do you think we shall find Leonard Parks alive, George?"

George Mason was a bit taken aback at the bluntness of the question.

"Hard to figure, at this juncture," he considered. "I should say the odds are fifty-fifty at best. I rang Justine Parks again when we reached Vienna, to check if he had been in touch with her since we left Zurich. She has heard nothing. And this secret society aspect only complicates matters."

"Do you think the Potenti might have eliminated him?" Alison then asked.

"Whatever makes you say that?"

"For his pursuit of Professor Jarvis, of course."

"Now you are way ahead of me, Alison" her colleague said. "Unless, of course, Jarvis was into something so deep that his exposure threatened a whole bunch of interests."

"Aren't both he and Leonard Parks members of the same society?"

"The tax investigator would have recognized Jarvis as a member of the Potenti, almost certainly in my view. The coat of arms on his study desk was a complete give-away. But whether the reverse is true, that the professor was aware of Parks' membership, is open to question. Dieter Lutz seemed to think that the two branches of the society operated independently."

"Much like branches of the secret service," Alison remarked, "as I pointed out earlier."

"Quite so, Alison!" Mason replied. "Perhaps the professor feared that Leonard Parks' enquiries into his tax status and his off-shore account would compromise certain of his activities. That might be sufficient reason to remove him from the scene."

"Jarvis would need to be pretty ruthless to do that, George," his colleague countered. "He did not strike me that way at all. More a typical ivory-tower academic."

"It is just a theory," George Mason replied. "And there is no harm whatsoever in theorizing. It is what our job comes down to, in the end, especially as regards motives. But come now, let us finish our drinks and see if we can locate this museum."

So saying, they settled their bill and set off at a fairly brisk pace despite the afternoon heat, winding their way through the narrow alleys of the Belvaros and taking a few wrong turns, before entering the spacious premises of the National Gallery. The cool air of the interior greeted them like a caress. They spent an agreeable couple of hours admiring the exhibits, mainly the paintings and the sculptures, until Alison Aubrey decided she had seen enough for one day. George Mason would have liked to view the panel paintings and the historic altar-pieces too, over in a separate wing of the building, but he deferred to the young woman's wish to return to the hotel to rest for a while and freshen up. One could have a surfeit of fine art, he mused, much as one could of haute cuisine. Best to take it in digestible amounts. To avoid the afternoon heat, they took a tram the length of Andrassy Street, with the feeling almost of being regular denizens of the Hungarian capital.

Alighting at a stop close to their hotel, they arranged to meet up again in the foyer at six o'clock. Mason had already spotted an appealing-looking restaurant, the Bela, recommended in his guidebook for Hungarian cuisine. It was just two blocks away.

On entering his room, he again dialed Milos Foldes' telephone number, without success. Stretching out on the divan bed, he switched on the television by remote control and, by trial and error, found an international news channel. Although he understood nothing of the commentary, he sat bolt upright as he recognized the backdrop. It was unmistakably Zell University campus, with the lake and the Kitzsteinhorn clearly visible in the background. The reporter was interviewing a girl, most likely a student, shown standing next to a ruddy-faced older man, probably her father. They were speaking in a language unfamiliar to him; which could have been Serbo-Croat, dubbed in German for the Austrian public. It was too quick for him to catch anything more than the general sense. Could this be the young woman, he wondered, whose kidnapping he had read about in *Wiener Abendblatt* two days ago? If so, there she was, hale and hearty and apparently none the worse for wear. A sum of money was mentioned. It seemed clear to him that a ransom had been paid, with the police kept at arm's length. He had mixed feelings about that, as the television program switched from Zell to Salzburg, for a report on equestrianism.

He was aroused an hour later by a loud rapping on his bedroom door. Getting slowly to his feet, he realized that he had fallen asleep. Crossing the parquet floor, he opened the door to find Alison Aubrey regarding him with some concern.

"You all right, George?" she anxiously enquired.

"What time is it, Alison?"

"Six-twenty. I have been waiting for you in the foyer."

"Sorry," he said, "Must have dozed off after the afternoon's exertions. Give me a few minutes and I shall be right down."

Closing the door, he went to the bathroom to freshen up. He then crossed to the telephone and dialed the same Budapest number he had tried on arrival in Budapest. In a few moments, to his relief, the line became live.

"Milos Foldes."

"Good evening, Mr. Foldes," the detective began. "My name is George Mason. I am ringing you on behalf of Justine Parks."

"Leonard's wife!" the surprised Hungarian exclaimed. "Is there some kind of problem?"

"I was hoping to speak to you about that. This very evening, if convenient."

"Where are you now, may I ask?"

"At my hotel on Andrassy Street. We are about to leave for an early dinner at the Bela, just a few blocks from here."

"You said *we*. You are not alone?" Foldes guardedly asked.

"I am with my assistant, Alison Aubrey."

The presence of a woman seemed to reassure the Hungarian.

"I know the Bela," he said. "I shall pick you up directly outside at eight o'clock sharp. That should give you enough time to appreciate our local cuisine, given that the service there can be rather slow."

"Until later, then," the detective said, jubilantly ringing off.

Replacing the receiver, he grabbed his jacket and hurried

downstairs to the brightly-lit foyer, where Alison was patiently waiting. Since they had skipped lunch, they found they had a good appetite by the time they reached the restaurant, settling down at a corner table under soft lights to listen to a violinist playing gipsy music. Conferring with his companion, Mason ordered a double serving of pirakas, a rich lamb stew seasoned with sweet paprika, which was some twenty minutes in preparation. When it finally arrived, served by a waitress in folk costume, they allowed a few minutes for it to cool, before tackling it, helping it down with a bottle of Bull's Blood. By the time they had taken dessert, it was approaching the hour of eight. Milos Foldes' car, a vintage Opel, was already parked at the curb as they stepped outside. A slim individual in his mid-forties, with dark eyes and tousled hair and wearing an open-neck shirt with jeans, emerged to greet them.

"George Mason?" he enquired.

"Guilty," the detective said, clasping the outstretched hand. "And this is my colleague, Alison Aubrey."

The Hungarian bowed slightly towards her with old-world courtesy, opening the rear door of the sedan for her to step inside. Mason walked round to the front passenger seat and fastened his seat-belt, as the driver accelerated towards the river. Within minutes, he drew up outside a modern apartment block on the embankment, hopped out to assist his guests and led them up several flights of steps to his quarters on the top floor. George Mason was a little out of breath by the time they were shown into a spacious apartment-cum-studio, starkly modern in décor. Milos led them first to the picture windows, which gave a panoramic view of the Danube, before inviting them to sit on high stools at the marble-topped counter and offering them drinks.

"I would prefer coffee," George Mason said, aiming to keep a clear head.

"Just a mineral water for me," Alison requested.

"Be my guests," Milos declared, returning minutes later from the small kitchen with Turkish coffee and a bottle of Magyar Spring water.

Mason was eyeing the photographic equipment everywhere in evidence, while Alison had stepped across to the opposite wall, which was almost completely covered with framed photographs.

Noting their interest, Milos said:

"Photography is my profession. I take views, mainly of the surrounding countryside, the Carpathians and the Danube environs, for the tourist trade. Souvenir shops and several modern art galleries stock my work."

"It looks very accomplished," an impressed Alison Aubrey remarked.

Their host had a diffident streak, seeming a little taken aback at such candid praise.

"They help keep body and soul together," he modestly replied, pouring himself a glass of red wine.

"And this is where you live year-round?" Mason asked. "I envy you the view."

"It is much better now," Milos replied, "than it was in my youth, under Communism. The city has blossomed and found its true ethos again. There is music in the air, and an almost palpable lightness of spirit."

"We had a taste of that at the Bela," Alison remarked. "They played gipsy melodies."

"But, rewarding as it is," Milos continued, "you did not both come here to absorb the local culture. You said you were acquainted with Justine Parks, so you must also have known my good friend Leonard?"

"Actually, no," Mason replied, a little awkwardly. "Let us put our cards on the table. Alison and I are detectives from Scotland Yard. We have never personally met Leonard Parks. We are here at the behest of Justine Parks because her husband has gone missing on what was supposedly a routine series of tax investigations."

"You mean that Leonard did not arrive back in England after leaving Budapest?" Milos asked, as much concerned as surprised.

"You can confirm that he was here in Budapest?"

"Absolutely," the other replied. "He stayed for two days right here in this apartment. We reminisced about old times. We were students together in the twilight years of the Communist regime. Things were beginning to loosen up a little and talk of change was in the air. It was an exciting time. We frequented the cafes to play chess and hold frank discussions about politics, without fear of betrayal by informers."

"Was Leonard Parks part of all that?" Alison Aubrey asked him.

"He was one of the leading lights," Milos claimed. "He also got involved in assisting refugees from East Germany when they began filtering across the border. After university, as the economy was beginning to privatize, he joined the staff of an insurance company. I think his main role there was to investigate bogus claims."

"A useful background," Mason judiciously remarked, "for his current post with the U.K. Inland Revenue."

"Which he was very pleased to accept," the photographer said, "following his marriage to Justine. It presented him with just the right sort of opportunity to establish himself in England."

"All very interesting," Mason said. "But tell me, Milos,

what was his state of mind while he was here in Budapest? We have traced his movements since he left England and met with everyone he interviewed, in Ostend, Zurich and Zell. Everything seems to have gone more or less according to plan."

"Frankly, Mr. Mason," Milos remarked, "I was a bit worried about him by the end of his visit. He seemed very preoccupied on that final evening and spoke little. The next day, I flew to Switzerland to attend the Lugano Biennale, a convention for graphic artists, photographers and book illustrators. Leonard intended to sleep late, saying he would let himself out. He told me not to be concerned and that he would be in touch. I was a bit reluctant to leave him, to tell you the truth, but I had no alternative."

"Did he mention what his plans were for that day?" Alison Aubrey asked.

"He said he intended to take a mini-cruise on the Danube, to Visegrad, to give him time to think things over."

"He had a lot on his mind?" Mason prodded.

"I think he had a conflict of loyalties," Milos replied. "He fully intended to pursue a prominent academic - he would not reveal the man's name - regarding income salted away in a tax haven. It was to be the highlight of his trip to Europe and seemed to mean a lot for his career prospects."

"I may know the individual you are referring to," the detective said, without mentioning Professor Jarvis by name.

"But apparently," the Hungarian continued, "Leonard decided that he could not pursue his investigations further. He mentioned personal reasons."

"Did he give you any clue as to what those reasons might be?" Alison asked.

"None whatsoever, Mademoiselle, and I did not wish to pry. I was more concerned about his heavy drinking."

"So that was the last time you saw him," Alison said, "the night before you left for Lugano?"

"Correct," the other replied. "He was still sound asleep when I left in the early morning."

"I think that is all we need to know for the present," George Mason said, rising to his feet.

"I shall give both of you a lift back to your hotel," Milos offered. "Oh, and by the way, I have a recent snapshot of Leonard that might assist you at some point."

He crossed to his desk and returned with a color photograph taken in front of a local monument. He passed it to the detective, who recognized the sculpture as a mounted statue of St. Stephen, the country's patron saint.

"He looks in fine fettle," Mason remarked.

"That was taken on his first day here," the other explained, "when he was overjoyed to meet me again."

Mason showed it briefly to Alison, who peered closely at it, before handing it back.

"Since it is a fine evening," he said, "I think we would both prefer to walk off a rather heavy dinner. We shall be in touch with you again, Mr. Foldes, in the event of developments."

"Do not hesitate to contact me if I can be of further help," Milos said, showing his visitors out. "Leonard is an old and valued friend of mine."

The Scotland Yard pair strolled back along Andrassy Street towards their hotel in the balmy evening air, mingling with pedestrians seemingly relaxed and contented in the new era of democratic freedoms, much like the citizens of any other West European capital. Alison Aubrey remarked on how well-stocked the stores seemed, and on the quality of goods on display; whereas George Mason was more intrigued by the vibrant café life, and the gipsy music, both of which spilled over onto the sidewalks.

"Interesting, don't you think," he said, distracting his companion from a gown shop window, "Milos' remark about his friend's heavy drinking?"

"*Very*," Alison emphasized. "What weight do you give, George, to his notion that Leonard Parks was experiencing a conflict of loyalties?"

"It could be highly significant," her colleague replied, "and perhaps even the key to this whole mystery. But we shall not know anything for sure until we contact Justine again."

"Although Milos did not say as much, since he was unaware of all the facts, I got the firm impression that Parks may have baulked at publicly exposing a leading member of the Potenti."

"Very astute of you, Alison," Mason remarked. "It was my reaction, too, as a matter of fact. The unanswered question now is whether Leonard Parks could live with such a conflict of loyalties, in view of his obligations to the Inland Revenue and the significant career implications that would have."

"I do hope, George," Alison said, "that you are not thinking what I am thinking."

"That the burden was too much for him and he has somehow harmed himself?"

"Heavy drinking could be a pointer in that direction," she suggested. "I have come across several cases, even in my short career, where people hit the bottle before cracking up completely."

George Mason, well-aware of human weaknesses, returned a philosophical smile. He said nothing, preferring to keep his thoughts to himself. As soon as he reached his room, having bade a rather weary Sergeant Aubrey good-night, he placed a call to Balderstones, hoping that Leonard's wife was not away at one of the village bridge evenings.

"Justine Parks," came a rather hesitant voice over the line.

"Good evening, Justine. George Mason here."

"Good to hear from you again, Inspector!" she exclaimed, glad to greet an ally. "Where are you speaking from now?"

"From my hotel in Budapest."

"You have covered a lot of ground already," Justine said. "You surely have some news?" There was a hint of optimism in her voice.

"Afraid not, so far," the detective replied. "We just came from a meeting with his old college friend, Milos Foldes. He remarked among other things, I regret to say, that your husband was drinking heavily."

There was a pause, as Justine absorbed this unexpected and troubling piece of information.

"That is not like Leonard at all," she said, moments later. "He has always been a social drinker, at least since I have known him. Just a few rounds with friends and neighbors at the village pub, or a glass of wine with dinner."

"No history of alcohol abuse?" Mason pointedly asked.

"None whatsoever," she emphatically replied.

"Then there must have been a good reason for it," the detective said. "Tell me, how important was this European assignment to him, in terms of his career?"

"A Superintendent Maitland rang me recently, to ask me the very same question," Justine replied.

How curious, the detective thought, that James Maitland

should be poking his nose into things at this juncture.

"And what did you tell him?" he asked.

"I told him the same as I am now telling you," she replied, "that Leonard set great store by it and was hoping to obtain a promotion on the strength of it."

"A lack of success would have weighed heavily on his mind?"

"Absolutely," Justine replied. "He would have considered that he had let his employers down, as well as himself. He was determined to justify the Inland Revenue's confidence in him."

"I think, Justine," George Mason tentatively remarked, "that your husband may have had some difficulty with one of his cases. It may, in fact, have compromised the success of his mission."

"Which tax dodger would you be referring to?" Justine indignantly enquired.

"I am not at liberty to say," the detective replied. "For the time being, it is just a working hypothesis. But it might explain your husband Leonard's uncharacteristic bout of heavy drinking."

There was silence again at the other end of the line, as if Justine was considering all the angles. After a few moments, she said:

"You may very well be correct in your supposition, Inspector Mason. I am not really in a position to judge. But since my husband is evidently still missing, please tell me what you intend to do now. I am entirely in your hands."

"Detective Sergeant Aubrey and I are proceeding with our enquiries," George Mason reassured her. "Leonard was fine when Milos Foldes left him to fly to a convention at Lugano, and we do have some new leads. We take up the trail again tomorrow morning."

"It has been four weeks now," Justine said, "since I last heard from my husband. I am beginning to have serious misgivings."

George Mason swallowed hard and repressed the urge to mention either murder or suicide as possible scenarios. There was simply not enough hard evidence at this stage to support either outcome.

"Whatever you do, Justine," he urged, "you must not give up hope."

"I shall ring his mother at Zurich," she replied, resignedly, "just on the off-chance Leonard has made recent contact with her."

"Give Léni Farkas my regards," he said, ringing off. "And take good care of yourself."

CHAPTER TEN

Immediately after breakfast on the following day, the Scotland Yard agents took a cab to Keleti Station, having little to go on beyond Milos Foldes' assertion that his friend Leonard Parks had intended to take a mini-cruise to Visegrad, to think through his situation. After nearly four weeks had lapsed, they were hoping it would still be possible to pick up traces of the missing tax investigator, by enquiring at the riverside towns between Budapest and Visegrad. At Keleti Information Desk, Mason obtained a route map and purchased tourist passes enabling them to break their journey at any point along the route. That done, they bought bottled water and boarded the regional train service to the Austrian border. It ran close to the northern bank of the Danube, speeding through picturesque villages before coming to a halt one hour later at Szentendre, where they alighted. Emerging from the country station, they found themselves in a charming cobbled square fronted by cafes, shops and the elegant homes of former merchants. The scene was dominated by a large stone cross, which on closer examination they found had been erected to mark the bubonic plague, the same pestilence that had swept at various times through most European countries, including England, wiping out a third of the population. It was known as the Black Death.

A police officer was doing his rounds, checking on local businesses in that relaxed, friendly manner law enforcement often enjoys in quiet country towns. George Mason, employing his rather rusty German, a sort of *lingua franca* throughout Eastern Europe, enquired of him the location of police headquarters. He was informed that it was situated in a narrow street leading off the main square, in a half-timbered building that had formerly been a ship chandler's home. The officer-in-charge, who had never previously received visitors from Scotland Yard, was agreeably surprised to see them, leading them into a meeting room at the rear of the building and offering them Turkish coffee.

"What can I do for you?" Kapitan Gulyas helpfully asked, once formalities were concluded.

George Mason produced the photograph of Leonard Parks that Milos had given him, but it was soon obvious that the officer did not recognize him.

"He supposedly came this way by river boat," the detective explained, "two or three weeks ago."

"And what was his reason for visiting Hungary?" the officer asked.

"He is an investigator for the Inland Revenue in Britain," Alison Aubrey explained. "He was on the trail of British expatriates suspected of evading their tax liabilities."

Kapitan Gulyas returned a knowing smile.

"In that case," he said, "he may have fallen foul of the local mafia. They have a hand in most financial dealings, especially those below the radar of the law."

"You are referring, Kapitan," Alison remarked, "to narcotics, money laundering, ransoms, that sort of thing?"

"The whole gamut," the officer replied, "including tax

scams. You name it, they are into it. Fortunately, they are not much in evidence on my watch. Szentendre is, on the whole, a very law-abiding place."

"Supposing Mr. Parks met with an accident of some sort," Mason said, trying to keep his hopes alive for Justine's sake. "Is there a local hospital we could check?"

The officer regretfully shook his head.

"The nearest hospital is in Vacs," he replied, "which is the next town higher up the Danube. But I can contact the local morgue on your behalf, if you so wish."

George Mason exchanged uneasy glances with his colleague, who reluctantly nodded her assent. Kapitan Gulyas then picked up the phone, dialed and spoke rapidly in his native tongue. After a few minutes, he replaced the receiver, shrugged his broad shoulders and said:

"There is no one fitting that description currently in the morgue. I asked them particularly to check for crime victims and possible drownings, but all they have had in recent weeks are elderly local residents who died of natural causes. Perhaps you should make further enquiries at Vacs?"

"We intend to do just that," Mason said, draining the strong coffee and rising to his feet. Alison followed suit.

The officer accompanied them to the front office.

"What I could do for you," he suggested, "is have posters made from your photograph and circulate them to all police stations in the Budapest hinterland. It will take a few days, but it may produce results."

"That would be most helpful of you," the detective said, passing him the photograph again so that he could take a color print on the office machine.

"Good day to you both," he said, on completing this task. "And good luck."

It was past midday when they arrived in Vacs, having waited thirty minutes at Szentendre station for the next train service. As they stood on the platform watching an express rattle through, George Mason figured that this must be the route of the old Orient Express, from Vienna to Istanbul, as evoked in novels by Agatha Christie and Graham Greene. He remarked as much to his colleague, who was quite intrigued by the literary associations. She had never read Greene's *Stamboul Train*, but had enjoyed the film *Murder on the Orient Express,* based on the Agatha Christie novel, with Hercule Poirot as the sleuth.

They found that Vacs was a much larger town than Szentendre, dominated by a medieval castle built by Crusaders against incursions of the Turks. Strolling through the Baroque main square past the cathedral, they followed a sign to the hospital which led them down to a promenade along the river embankment, where they paused for a light lunch at one of the riverside restaurants patronized mainly by local residents and small groups of elderly German tourists. If George Mason had half expected to bump into someone fitting his mental image of Leonard Parks, on the grounds that the latter had decided to lie low for a while in some provincial Hungarian town, he was disappointed, but not surprised. He realized that he was letting his native optimism gain the upper hand, regarding the fate of the taxman who, he reluctantly acknowledged, may no longer be among the living. Alison Aubrey, noting his preoccupied air, ate her prawn sandwich in silence, while observing with keen interest the activity on the fast-flowing river. In addition to the occasional passenger vessel, there was a constant stream of barges and small freighters.

"The Danube must be one of the main commercial arteries in Europe," she remarked, as they at length continued their walk, "judging by the volume of traffic."

"As it has been, I imagine, since Roman times," Mason replied. "They would have shipped wine, olive oil, grains and livestock down to the coast, to be ferried by sea to outposts of the Roman Empire."

"Like re-living history in a way, isn't it, George?" she enthused.

"Few places better for it," he remarked, "with Romans, Magyars, Turks, Crusaders, Nazis and the Soviets all coming this way at one time or another, leaving their distinctive mark on it. I imagine Vacs has seen more than its share of upheavals in its day."

"It seems peaceful enough now, *and* quite prosperous," Alison said.

"Because it is enjoying, probably for the first time in a long and varied history, the benefits of democracy, the rule of law and free enterprise," George Mason was quick to point out.

Their promenade route brought them, within twenty minutes, to the main entrance of the hospital, set some way back from the river in its own spacious grounds. They entered and approached Enquiries, where Mason explained his mission as best as he could in German. The registrar seemed to understand and bade an auxiliary worker lead them down a side corridor to the Emergency Room. The duty nurse, an agile man in his mid-thirties, sprang forward to meet them. They showed him the photograph, which he studied carefully.

"I know this man," he said, almost immediately. "Or someone who looks very much like him."

"Who was admitted to this hospital?" Mason quickly asked.

"A short time ago," the nurse explained, "a man fitting

147

this description was fished out of the river and brought here by two bargemen. They claimed to have spotted him near one of the passenger vessels. But they could not say whether he jumped or fell."

The two detectives exchanged concerned looks.

"Did the man in question survive the experience?" Alison immediately asked.

The nurse nodded affirmatively and handed back the photograph.

"He was in bad shape," he replied, "from swallowing river water. But we managed to pull him round in the end."

"Did he give you his name?" George Mason asked, inwardly elated at the thought that, if they were in fact discussing the tax investigator, he was most likely still alive. Such knowledge would be music to Justine's ears, not to mention his mother's.

"I am afraid not," the other said. "The patient was suffering from amnesia, either as a result of striking his head against an object in the water, or as a result of heavy drinking. His blood alcohol level was abnormally high."

"What about personal effects, such as his passport, wallet or driver's license?" the detective asked.

"None of those items was recovered," the helpful nurse replied. "They could have been washed into the river or removed from his person by the same bargemen who rescued him."

"Could we trace the barge in question?" George Mason wanted to know.

"Virtually impossible, I would say," came the quick reply. "There are so many craft plying the Danube, you understand, in either direction. They could be at the Black Sea by now, or at some port in Austria, Hungary or Romania."

"So you really have no confirmation of the man's identity?" Mason asked in some surprise.

"There was one object that did survive the incident," the other replied. "He was wearing a small brass locket, of little intrinsic value, on a chain round his neck. We opened it, seeking a clue to his identity."

"And what did it reveal?" Alison eagerly enquired.

"Not a great deal," the nurse replied. "Certainly not a name. The inside face of the locket, in common with many similar objects, showed the image of a saint. Opposite the image was a telephone number, which we thought might be some kind of helpline in case of personal difficulty or distress."

"So you rang that number?" George Mason prompted.

"We did indeed, mainly to help establish an identity. Or, at the very least, to contact a next of kin."

"And did you succeed?" the detective asked, knowing full well that nobody had contacted Justine about her husband's whereabouts.

"Much to our surprise," the nurse said, "and to our pleasant surprise, I might add, our telephone call reached the central exchange of a monastic order called the Vespertines. We explained the situation to them. Two days later, three men in dark-gray habits, who represented themselves to us as monk-hospitalers, arrived here in a small ambulance. It was a modern vehicle, as I recall it, with state-of-the-art equipment such as paramedics use."

"So you passed your patient into their care?" Mason asked, now reasonably sure they were discussing Leonard Parks.

"The monks explained that they were developing new, experimental therapies for treating amnesiacs; whereas our resources and expertise in that area are rather limited. Our medical director, Dr. Ferenc, was more than happy to hand the subject over to them."

"Weren't you running a risk," Alison queried, "in taking these monks at their word, just like that, without checking their credentials?"

The young nurse reacted with indignation.

"Hungary is a Catholic country," he maintained. "We are not accustomed to questioning the authenticity or sincerity of our priests, monks and nuns."

"Of course not," Mason said, aiming to smooth matters over. "Then we can take it that the patient was sufficiently recovered, at least as to his physical condition, to withstand the transfer?"

"He was still rather weak," the other replied. "But the monks assured us they would take especially good care of him. We saw no reason to doubt their word, in view of their advanced medical equipment."

"Did the patient say anything at all during the few days he was in your care?"

"Hold on a minute," the duty nurse said, stepping towards a small office in the corner of the Emergency Room.

"This is beginning to look promising," Mason remarked to his colleague.

Within a few moments, the man returned with a slip of paper.

"After he had partially recovered from his near-drowning," he said, "the patient entered a state of delirium which lasted most of his second day with us. He repeated these words over and over. They seemed so unconventional and unexpected that I wrote them down, in case they might have some significance."

George Mason eagerly took the slip of paper and read

aloud the words *Feci quod potui.*

"Latin," he said, in puzzlement. "Do you know what it means?"

The nurse regretfully shook his head.

"I showed it to the hospital chaplain," he explained. "He too recognized it as Latin, but he did not know what it meant either."

"Rather surprising," Alison observed. "Perhaps they do not teach Latin any more in the seminaries, since church services are nowadays conducted in the vernacular."

"There are still some devotees of the Latin mass," Mason interposed, "in more conservative circles of the Roman Church."

The nurse nodded agreement.

"They say an early-morning mass in Latin once a month at Vacs cathedral," he told them, "for the benefit of traditionalists."

"But your chaplain is evidently not one of them," Alison pointedly remarked.

"I am afraid not," came the reply. "Fr. Antonin is a young priest, of the more modern, post-Vatican 2 school."

"May we take this slip of paper?" Mason asked. "I know someone who may be able to make something of it." He had in mind a certain antiquarian bookseller at Schipfe, Zurich.

"By all means," the nurse replied. "It is of no further use to us."

The visitors thanked him warmly and left the hospital, making their way through the well-kempt grounds and along the riverside promenade, back towards the center of the town.

"What do you make of all that, George?" Alison asked him.

"At least," he buoyantly replied, "it seems that Leonard Parks may well be still alive, and nobody will be more pleased to hear that than Justine Parks. As to his going overboard, the question arises as to whether he had simply drunk too much and lost his balance; or whether he made a suicide bid. Either way, it indicates that he was under a great deal of stress."

"You are ruling out attempted murder?"

George Mason walked on in silence for a while, weighing Alison's challenging question. He kept one eye on the heavily-laden barges plying down-river, which seemed to be freighting mainly coal and timber.

"If you are suggesting that some person or persons aboard that boat shoved him," he said eventually, "I agree that must remain one of several possibilities, but we have no means of verifying it. Our brief is merely to trace Leonard Parks, not to nail would-be assassins. That task, if relevant, would be a matter for the local police."

"You are right, of course," his young colleague admitted. "So what do you make of those Latin words?"

"They mean nothing to me," he replied, "since I did not take Latin at school."

"Nor did I," Alison admitted.

"But I shall discover their precise meaning in due course," he continued. "If Leonard Parks kept repeating them in his delirium, while recalling nothing else from his past, not even his own name, they must hold special significance for him."

"The locket he was wearing," Alison said, "contained the image of a saint, according to the duty nurse. Which saint do you think it might be?"

"My best guess," the detective artfully replied, "would be St. Kasimir. And it would not surprise me at all if our subject is not now residing at a certain priory in Glarus, courtesy of the Vespertine Order. I somehow doubt, however, that they will be trying to cure his amnesia."

Alison Aubrey gave him a curious sideways glance, not quite sure what he was getting at, as they reached the main square of Vacs, thronging with visitors to the historic sites and outdoor restaurants. The sky had clouded over and seemed to threaten rain. Noting the fact, the detective said:

"Perhaps we should get back to Budapest without delay, check out of our hotel and catch the evening train to Vienna."

"What about food?" Alison asked. The walk to and from the hospital had piqued her appetite.

"How about dinner on the train?" Mason suggested. "They have excellent dining-cars on these international services."

"Sounds like a great idea, George," she replied. "It will be like traveling on the fabled Orient Express."

"You bet," he smilingly rejoined.

*

Around the same time that George Mason and Alison Aubrey were taking their seats in the dining-car of the *Enesco*, a Pullman express from Bucharest to Vienna calling at Budapest, Sir Maurice Weeks, First Secretary at the Exchequer, entered the spacious lounge of the Royal Hunt Hotel at Putney Bridge, south of the Thames. Occupying a stool at a secluded corner of the bar, he ordered a glass of Flower's Bitter and cast a keen eye over the room. It was half full of members of the local stockbroker belt and similar well-heeled patrons enjoying a quiet drink before dinner. He recognized a few of them, but chose not to fraternize with them on this occasion, having other things on his mind. Minutes later, he was joined by Superintendent James Maitland, of the Metropolitan Police.

"What will you have, Jim?" he enquired.

"Scotch-and-soda," Maitland promptly replied, perching on an adjacent stool and glancing guardedly round the room.

"Cheers," the former said, the minute the whisky was served.

"Your very good health, Sir Maurice," Maitland responded.

"Aristide Lebrun, head of the French Chapter, tells me," Weeks continued, "that funds have now been transferred to the appropriate quarter to secure the nomination of our candidate for Finance Commissioner. An official announcement from Brussels, he assures me, should be made within the next two weeks."

Maitland slowly sipped his drink, aware that 'transfer to the appropriate quarter' meant that the bribe had been offered and accepted.

"It means," he confidently asserted, "that the Potenti will control a key office of the European Commission. We can soon begin fully to implement our program and reverse decades of socialist and welfare programs. Europe will be the fitter and leaner for it. But how can you be sure, Sir Maurice, that the European Parliament at Strasbourg will ratify the new agenda?"

The civil servant thoughtfully weighed the question for a few moments, while nudging his glass towards the barman for a refill.

"Right-wing parties now hold the balance of power at Strasbourg," he said, "especially after the recent series of elections. They will play along with any reduction in entitlements and kindred expenditures, since most of the far-right parties would like to limit the role of the Brussels bureaucracy in any case, in favor of greater autonomy for their home governments.

"What about left-wing politicians, Sir Maurice?" James Maitland then asked. "How will they react to cuts in welfare programs?"

"The leader of the Italian communists, Ettore Bianchi, is the main threat from the left," the civil servant replied, with a disdainful look.

"Wasn't he one of those politicians cited for tax evasion in Italy?" Maitland asked.

"I believe he was," Weeks smugly replied. "If I remember rightly, his name appeared in a list of clients of a private Swiss bank, revealed by a whistle-blower earlier this year. He will be very lucky to retain his seat. With Bianchi out of the way, we can be fairly confident the European Parliament will rubber-stamp our society's initiatives, with minimal debate. It will be up to Aristide Lebrun and his associates to engineer that result, while we British concentrate our efforts on securing control of the International Monetary Fund."

"No doubt, you are right," his companion agreed, impressed as ever with the First Secretary's political acumen.

In fairly buoyant mood, the two men finished their drinks while engaging in light conversation and pointing out to each other people they knew in the lounge bar, including personnel from other government departments. As the hands of the wall clock moved towards seven, they began to think in terms of dinner.

"Assure me of one thing, Jim," Sir Maurice said, "before we go through to the dining-room."

James Maitland returned a quizzical look, not quite sure what to expect.

"You do not foresee any snags, do you?" Weeks continued. "Anything that could go wrong at the last minute?"

The police superintendent smiled reassuringly.

"The only possible gray area," he replied, "has already been accounted for."

"And what might that be?" Sir Maurice immediately asked.

"We have taken the only uncertain factor out of the equation."

"Which is?"

"Leonard Parks," Maitland replied. "An agent of the Inland Revenue."

"You mentioned him before," Weeks said, "as a member of our junior branch, the Diligenti. Is it possible that you now doubt his loyalty?"

The police official's face clouded. He took a sip of his whisky and said:

"Difficult to know at this point, Sir Maurice. He was interviewing Paul Jarvis at Zell University regarding tax evasion. As you know, Professor Jarvis controls our main account in the Cayman Islands. It would be a disaster for our society if he were to be exposed and prosecuted in the courts. Our whole edifice could come crashing down."

The civil servant swallowed hard before saying:

"This could be very serious, Jim. Where do Leonard Parks' main loyalties lie? I should have thought that, as a member of the Diligenti, he would be unquestionably loyal to the society and its principle of *Omerta*."

"One would certainly hope that would be the case," the other replied. "I did, however, take the step of contacting his wife, Justine. She told me that success in his current round of investigations meant a great deal to her husband, and that a promotion hung on it. Having moved to England after their marriage, he was very keen to succeed and gain advancement in his chosen field."

"So there could well be a question mark against his loyalty to us," Weeks judiciously considered. "But you say that you have taken good care of things?"

"A completely fortuitous turn of events," the superintendent replied, "played right into our hands."

"Please do go on," the civil servant urged, steering his friend towards the dining-room, where he was contemplating the chef's evening special of stuffed turbot with baked potato and asparagus tips.

"It seems that Leonard Parks suffered some kind of mishap while aboard a passenger vessel on the Danube," Maitland explained. "He was fished out of the river by bargemen, who took him to the nearest hospital, at a place named Vacs."

"Where on earth is that, Jim?" a bemused Sir Maurice asked.

"Somewhere between Budapest and Vienna," his friend said. "Parks was found to be suffering from amnesia, most likely of a temporary nature. He could give the hospital staff no clue to his identity. His passport and other ID were apparently either lost in the river or stolen."

"That is quite a lucky break for us," the First Secretary said. "He will have forgotten all about Professor Paul Jarvis, at least for the foreseeable future."

"Also fortunate for us is the fact that he was wearing a St. Kasimir locket round his neck. The hospital administrator rang the helpline inscribed inside it. Three Vespertine monks promptly drove an ambulance to Vacs and persuaded the hospital to release him into their care. The director, a Dr. Ferenc, seemed perfectly O.K. with that."

The pair sat down at a quiet corner table and waived the menu aside, ordering the chef's special and a bottle of chilled Soave to help it down. Maurice Weeks mulled over in his mind the information he had just gleaned. After a while, he said:

"I thought you had a member of Special Branch on the Parks case?"

"Inspector George Mason," Maitland immediately replied.

"Since Leonard Parks is no longer missing, Jim, had you not better summon Inspector Mason back to England?"

"I will indeed do so, Sir Maurice, when I can contact him," the police official rather sheepishly replied.

"You mean he is not in regular contact with home base?" the civil servant asked, in some surprise.

"George Mason is something of a maverick," came the reply. "He likes to act the lone agent, and Chief Inspector Bill Harrington gives him plenty of rope, in view of his prior record. So on this occasion I took the precaution of assigning an assistant to him, a young detective sergeant named Alison Aubrey, who is counting on me to advance her career. She has rung me several times already, to keep me abreast of developments in the case. I am expecting another call any day now. I shall instruct her to tell Mason that the investigation is over, and that they are to return to London without delay."

"What reason shall you give," Maurice Weeks wanted to know, "without arousing his suspicions? It is better for our purposes if Leonard Parks remains out of circulation for the time being, in case he recovers his memory and decides that his main loyalties lie elsewhere, namely to the Inland Revenue."

"There is simply no way George Mason could discover Parks' present whereabouts," Maitland assured him. "The Vespertines are a highly reclusive order, with a number of discreet establishments across Europe. Some of them, rumor has it, may have been part of an underground network to help leading Nazis escape to South America in 1945. They will take good care of our Diligenti brother until such time as he recovers, leaving the healing process in the hands of Providence."

His dinner companion chuckled loudly at that last remark, implying as it did that the process of recovery would be a long-drawn-out affair, with little recuperative treatment provided by the monk-hospitalers.

"You think of everything, my dear fellow," he said, raising his glass. "To the Potenti!"

"*Faciant meliora potentes*," the other duly responded.

"Let those who can do better!"

CHAPTER ELEVEN

After arriving late in the Austrian capital and staying overnight at Hotel Graf, George Mason and Alison Aubrey went directly after breakfast the following morning to the Westbahnhof, to board the *Wiener Waltzer* back to Switzerland. Mason bought a copy of the London *Times*, to catch up on news about England; Alison preferred to enjoy the scenery and mull over events of the previous day. On arrival at the Graf, she ought really to have rung Superintendent Maitland to give him a progress report, but something had held her back. It had struck her, as they were rounding off a late dinner in the dining-car of the crack Budapest-Vienna express, that the initial letters of the Latin phrase the duty nurse at Vacs Hospital had shown them were vaguely familiar. On reaching her hotel room, after bidding her colleague good night, she had been on the point of ringing James Maitland when it suddenly occurred to her that the initial letters of *Feci quod potui,* the Latin words repeated over and over by Leonard Parks in his delirium, formed part of the superintendent's e-mail address he had used when confirming her assignment to accompany George Mason! She had made a note of the address in her diary: fqp.superjim@wideworld.com.

As the train gathered speed towards Linz, George

Mason, having checked his small portfolio of stocks and scanned the early soccer results of the new Premier League season, laid his newspaper aside for a moment and glanced across at his young colleague.

"You are very quiet this morning," he remarked.

"Just a little beat," Alison replied, "after all the excitement and running around of recent days."

"Care for a coffee?" he enquired, as the refreshment trolley trundled by.

She shook her head and glanced out of the carriage window, as Mason took up his reading again. She could hardly tell him, she considered, the real tenor of her thoughts that morning, but they hinged on loyalty. Her prime responsibility was undoubtedly to the superior officer, James Maitland; but the curious coincidence of a Latin phrase and an e-mail address made her wonder if, even though the notion seemed fantastic, the superintendent himself was not somehow connected to this strange secret society. An even more disturbing thought then crossed her mind. Was her presence on this assignment really for the benefit of her career, as the superintendent had represented it? Or was her main role to keep tabs on George Mason and report any progress he made back to London?

"A penny for your thoughts," George Mason said, glancing up again.

"Nothing in particular," she evasively replied. "Just wondering what lies ahead."

"We reach Ziegelbrucke in about five hours," he explained. "From there, it is a fairly short stretch by funicular railway to Glarus."

"A long trip," she replied, philosophically. "But I do not really mind, George. I quite enjoy rail travel."

"We could grab a sandwich from the trolley for a bite of

lunch to tide us over until dinner. Remember that old-world inn on the main street, Der Goldener Hirsch? We shall book in there for the night."

"I am looking forward to it," Alison said, deciding there and then that her first loyalty now lay with her genial and astute colleague sitting opposite. To hell with her career prospects for the time being; she would stand solidly behind George Mason until this investigation was concluded, omit to ring the superintendent and face whatever consequences might follow. For the time being, however, she preferred to keep her thoughts on these matters to herself.

The train passed in turn through Linz, Salzburg and Innsbruck, before entering the long, precipitous Arlberg Pass to reach the border with Switzerland. At 4.53 p.m. precisely, it pulled into Ziegelbrucke, where they alighted and caught the funicular railway to Glarus, arriving at Der Goldener Hirsch at just turned six o'clock. The innkeeper recognized them the moment they stepped inside.

"Back so soon?" he cordially remarked.

"We shall need rooms for the night," George Mason explained, "if you have vacancies."

"You are in luck," the innkeeper said. "We just had two cancellations; otherwise we would have been fully booked. They are superior rooms."

"We shall take them, regardless of cost," the detective said, unconcerned that he was already quite a bit over-budget.

The innkeeper registered them and showed them to separate rooms on the second floor, where they freshened up before meeting again in the restaurant. It was full of late-season tourists, in addition to attendees at a conference held that afternoon for tour promoters. Mason overheard

English voices at a nearby table and noticed lapel badges for Overland Tours, which he had a vague impression was based somewhere in the north of England. He refrained from introducing himself to his compatriots, however, to avoid arousing their curiosity regarding his presence at Glarus.

"We were lucky to find a spare table," Alison remarked, as they scanned the elaborate menu.

"Everybody and his brother seems to be in Glarus just now," Mason replied. "It seems to be the time for travel conferences, now that the main tourist season is over. Forward planning for next year, I should imagine."

With only two waiters to attend so many tables, service was inevitably slow. It was almost nine o'clock when they emerged from the inn after a hearty meal, to be kissed by the refreshingly-cool mountain air. Although it was already dusk, they took a stroll to the edge of town, as far as the bramble-strewn path that climbed up to the priory. There they stopped and gazed upwards, but no lights were visible. The crest of the hill was shrouded in darkness and silence, save for sporadic birdcall.

"Perhaps the monks use candles," Alison jocularly observed.

"That would not surprise me in the least," Mason rejoined, thinking he saw a faint glimmer of light at one of the upper windows.

"Do you really think we shall find Leonard Parks there tomorrow?" she asked, in a tone that conveyed a decided element of uncertainty.

"Where else would he be," George Mason quickly responded, "if he was placed in the care of the Vespertines?"

The young sergeant did not reply to what seemed a

rhetorical question, keeping her reservations to herself and hoping for her colleague's sake that his view was correct. She fell in step with him as he turned and walked, briskly for a man of his size, back to the inn, where he proposed a nightcap in the bar. The restaurant crowd had thinned by now, a log fire had been lit and an accordion player embarked on a medley of alpine tunes. There were compensations, she felt, to foreign assignments like this, hoping that she had not cooked her goose for future deployments by omitting to telephone the superintendent. Feeling suddenly weary from the long rail trip and the brisk evening walk, she retired within the hour, leaving a pensive George Mason nursing a pint of pilsner in the inglenook and gazing into the log fire, much as he might have done at his favorite pub back home.

The following morning they rose early and took breakfast before the party of tour promoters came down. By nine-thirty, they were inside Glarus Polizei Dienst, where they were shown into the office of Leutnant Ray Baer, the senior officer. He was surprised to see them.

"What brings Scotland Yard to this quiet neck of the woods?" he enquired, much intrigued.

"We have reason to believe," George Mason began, "that a fellow-countryman of ours, a Mr. Leonard Parks, is being held at St. Kasimir's Priory against his will."

"That is a very serious accusation, Inspector Mason," Baer guardedly remarked. "What grounds do you have for making it?"

"We have been trying to trace Mr. Parks," the detective continued, "for the past ten days. He was reported missing by his wife Justine, after he failed to contact her during a British government assignment to several European countries."

"A government agent, indeed?" the Swiss officer said. "That sounds serious. Can you enlarge on it?"

"Parks is an investigator for the Inland Revenue," Alison Aubrey explained, "chasing tax dodgers living abroad."

"But what grounds do you have for thinking this individual may now be at Glarus?"

"We traced him to a hospital at Vacs," Alison replied. "That is a Danube town between Budapest and Vienna."

"Was he ailing?" the lieutenant asked, with evident concern.

"It seems that he fell, or was pushed, from a passenger vessel on the river," Mason explained. "As a result, he is apparently suffering from amnesia. The hospital administrator, using a helpline number inscribed inside a locket Parks was wearing at the time, contacted the Vespertine Order. They sent monk-hospitalers in an ambulance to Vacs to collect him, on the grounds that they could help restore his memory. I am assuming they brought him here, to St. Kasimir's."

"Why would you think that?" the other dubiously enquired.

"Because Leonard Parks visited the priory on a side-trip from Zurich not very long ago. We think he is connected to it through a secret society known as the Potenti."

"Never heard of them," Ray Baer came back at once. "But since you seem so sure of your grounds, Inspector, and since you have come all this way from London, we shall do our level best to assist you. We shall drive up to the priory and make some enquiries."

"I doubt that the prior, Fr. Dominic, will admit to much," Mason said.

"We shall take a search warrant and go through the place with a fine toothcomb," the other assured him. "That will take time, mind you, Inspector Mason. It is a rambling old building, originally the cantonal governor's residence, completed in the eighteenth century." With a glance at Alison Aubrey, he added: "But they do not admit women."

The Scotland Yard pair exchanged ironic glances and shrugged, implying there was not much they could do about that.

"Take the morning off, Alison," Mason generously offered. "Explore the town center and the shops, have a coffee somewhere and meet me back at Der Goldener Hirsch for lunch. I expect we shall be through by noon."

"That is just fine by me," his young colleague emphatically replied. "I have no desire whatsoever to impinge on male chauvinism, whether in a priory, a London gentlemen's club, a boardroom, or anywhere else for that matter."

"So that is settled," the Swiss officer said, with a hearty laugh at her turn of phrase. "Give me ten minutes and I shall have a squad car waiting outside."

Back on the main street, Alison Aubrey took leave of her colleague and set off to make the most of her free morning; while George Mason waited for Leutnant Baer, who soon joined him accompanied by two junior officers. Minutes later, they were on their way to the priory by a narrow dirt road that wound steeply up the opposite side of the hill. The detective felt a keen sense of relief that he was spared another long climb up the bramble-strewn path.

"It certainly is news to me that there is a secret society operating here in Glarus," the lieutenant remarked, as their drive progressed. "Right under our very noses."

"Which is why it is secret," George Mason pointedly remarked. "So that outsiders, even people living in the neighborhood, would not know of its existence."

"Fair enough," Baer conceded. "And what are its objectives, Inspector Mason, in your considered opinion?"

"I have certain views about that, Leutnant," the detective replied. "But I prefer not to disclose them at the present time, pending further developments. You don't happen to know any Latin, I suppose?"

The Swiss officer firmly shook his head, while giving his English counterpart a baffled look for such an out-of-the-blue question. Aware that the English had a reputation for eccentricity, he began to wonder if this was not some kind of game he had allowed himself to get involved in. The Vespertines had excellent standing in the local community, mainly on account of their charitable works; they seemed to him the least likely people to be involved in the abduction of a government official. When the squad car reached the main building, he sprang out and grasped the bell-pull. A loud clang reverberated through the priory. Several minutes later, the heavy oaken door was partly opened by the same elderly cleric who had admitted George Mason on his previous visit. Leutnant Baer explained his mission and, after a deal of hesitation, the four police officers were finally admitted and shown into the reception room to await the prior. Minutes later, Fr. Dominic entered with a swish of his long habit, immediately recognizing both the police lieutenant and George Mason, turning from one to the other in evident concern.

"Leutnant Baer," he immediately asked, "to what do we owe the honor of a visit to our humble establishment?"

Baer put it to him as delicately as he could, deferring to his clerical status.

"We are seeking a certain individual, Father Prior," he explained, "who may quite recently have sought refuge here at St. Kasimir's."

The prior gave George Mason a mortified look.

"You were here some days ago, Inspector," he said, "seeking information about Leonard Farkas. I told you then that he passed through here very briefly, simply in order to visit his father's grave."

"There is a new development," the detective countered. "We have reason to believe that Leonard Parks, or Farkas if you prefer, was transferred here by ambulance from a hospital at Vacs, across the border with Hungary. The hospital administration claimed they had contacted your order using a telephone number inscribed inside a locket Mr Parks was wearing round his neck. The locket bore an image of St. Kasimir."

"That means absolutely nothing, Inspector," Fr. Dominic protested. "Kasimir is a popular saint, much venerated in these parts. Many people are accustomed to wearing such lockets, to ward off sickness or misfortune. "

"Are you saying that the ambulance did not originate here?" Alison Aubrey pressed.

"We have no medical facilities here whatsoever," the prior replied. "You have been misinformed. We have almoners, of course, who distribute aid to the poor, and members who sometimes assist the clergy in local parishes. Apart from that, we have no contact with the general public."

Ray Baer looked distinctly uncomfortable and unsure of his ground, as George Mason bluntly stated:

"We are here to conduct a search of these premises."

Fr. Dominic took a step backwards and gave the quartet of visitors a look of strong disapproval. An awkward silence followed, after which the lieutenant said:

"It is just a matter of routine, Father Prior, which should not take up too much time. I am confident that, if you claim that you are not harboring Mr. Parks, our search will be fruitless and we shall not need to disturb your quiet and orderly routine again."

The prior seemed a little mollified on hearing that, seeing in his compatriot a respectful son of the church, someone who respected the sanctity of hallowed ground.

"Please be as discreet as you can," he requested. "The brethren are reciting matins in the chapel. I am about to join them, if you will excuse me."

At that, the four police officers split up to comb the building, taking in the refectory, the sick bay, the library, the scriptorium and the dormitory. Just over an hour later, after conducting a thorough search while bypassing the chapel, out of respect, they met up again in the reception room, together with a bewildered George Mason. Matins over, the prior rejoined them.

"I am as concerned as you are, Herr Mason," Fr. Dominic remarked, with a glimmer of triumph in his otherwise inscrutable eye, "about the welfare of Leonard Farkas, son of the late, distinguished Count Farkas, especially if he has gone missing. But whatever information led you to believe that we might be harboring him here, presumably against his will, was seriously misguided, offensive even. Good day, gentlemen, and the Lord be with you. Brother Ambrosius will show you out."

"It would seem that you have been misled, Inspector," Ray Baer remarked, as the squad car eased its way back down the steep slope behind the priory. "How sure are you of your sources?"

"All I know, Leutnant, is that Leonard Parks was collected by three Vespertine monks from the public hospital at Vacs. I have the duty nurse's word on that."

"But as you saw for yourself, my dear sir, there are no

medical facilities at the priory, discounting the rudimentary sick bay for common or garden ailments such as the flu or gripe. How would they be sending out ambulances to retrieve persons suffering from conditions like amnesia, which call for a high degree of medical expertise?"

The English visitor reluctantly granted that his Swiss counterpart had a valid point. After a few moments' reflection, he said:

"Have you any information on similar foundations run by this same order?"

"None whatsoever," the other replied. "Religious orders seldom, if at all, come within the purview of the police. We tend to leave them to themselves, as they would doubtless wish to be. This will have to be an end to the matter, as far as my department is concerned. Can I drop you off somewhere, Inspector Mason?"

"A little farther along, at Der Goldener Hirsch," Mason replied, exiting the rear door of the sedan the moment it reached the inn. "My sincere apologies if you feel I have wasted your time."

"Do not even mention it, Inspector," Baer generously remarked. "If you had reasonable grounds for suspicion, it was as well to look into the matter, improbable as it seemed. Good luck with the course of your enquiries."

"Good day to you, Leutnant Baer," the detective said. "I am much obliged for the assistance you were able to give."

Alison Aubrey was patiently waiting for him on the narrow sidewalk, but she could tell from his expression that he had drawn a blank.

"Out of luck, I am afraid," he admitted, as they took their places at table for a spot of lunch. "Four of us combed every nook and cranny of that building, and you would be amazed at how labyrinthine it is. There was no sign of

Leonard Parks."

"What next?" Alison concernedly enquired.

"On to Zurich, by the early-afternoon train, to see if we can pick up the trail from there."

*

By late-afternoon, they were back on more familiar ground. After checking in again to Hotel Adler, they walked a short distance along the Limmat embankment, crossed the river to Schipfe and called at the antiquarian bookshop. Dieter Lutz was engaged in cataloging new stock, but did not seem particularly surprised to see them.

"Did you succeed in locating our missing friend?" he solicitously enquired.

"We have established that he is probably still among the living," Mason replied, "without discovering his precise whereabouts, except that he is most likely in the care - if that is the correct word - of the Vespertines. It seems that Leonard Parks may be suffering from amnesia, as a result of going overboard from a Danube riverboat."

"He had been drinking heavily," Detective Sergeant Aubrey added.

The bookseller thoughtfully stroked his chin.

"Alcohol abuse can trigger amnesia," he said, "as can a heavy blow to the head."

"While in the hospital at Vacs," Mason continued, "and in a state of delirium, he kept saying the same Latin words over and over. Neither my colleague nor I have any idea of what they signify, so I have been meaning to ask you, since you translated the Potenti motto for us when we were last here."

"*Faciant meliora potentes,*" Lutz recalled, with a self-satisfied chuckle. "Let those who can do better."

"How about *Feci quod potui?*" the detective asked.

The bookseller turned the phrase over in his mind for a few moments, a slow smile spreading across his astute features. He crossed to a shelf at the rear of the shop and took down what seemed to George Mason a dictionary of quotations. Flicking through it for a while and seemingly satisfied with his research, he put the volume back in its place and turned to his visitors. Just then, his telephone rang and he spent a few minutes discussing prices of his stock.

"Why did you consult a reference work?" an intrigued Alison Aubrey asked.

"It suddenly struck me," Dieter Lutz explained, "that the two phrases could be linked. I thought a quick check would decide the matter. They do in fact constitute a quotation from Pliny the Elder."

"Who on earth was that?" a baffled George Mason asked.

"A Roman naturalist and author," the antiquarian replied, "of the first century A.D."

"So the full quotation," an excited Alison said, "must be *Feci quod potui; faciant meliora potentes.*"

"Exactly so," Lutz confirmed. "Very elegant Latin it is, too, don't you agree?"

"But you still haven't explained the meaning," an impatient George Mason protested.

With a knowledgeable smile, the obliging bookseller said: "*I did what I could; let those who can do better.* Does that make you any wiser, Herr Mason?"

The perplexed detective shook his head.

"I wish I could say that it did," he wryly replied. "But I am afraid it means very little to me."

"But it obviously held great significance for Leonard Parks," Alison suggested. "Why else would he keep repeating it, while unable to recall even his own name?"

"You have a valid point there, Sergeant," her colleague admitted. "But short of him being here in person to explain its significance, I am afraid we must remain in the dark."

"It may have some bearing on the Potenti," the bookseller suggested. "If the second part of the quotation represents their motto, as shown on the coat of arms you saw at the priory, ask yourselves what the first part may refer to. Explore the possibilities. Use your imagination."

"We shall certainly give it a try," the bemused detective assured him.

"Now, if you will excuse me," Dieter Lutz said, "I have a deal of cataloging to catch up with before the annual audit. I do hope I have been of some genuine assistance to you both."

"Just one more thing," Mason said, turning back as he reached the door. "Do you happen to be aware of any other foundations, or facilities, in this country run by the Vespertine Order?"

The other regretfully shook his head.

"Not apart from St. Kasimir's," he replied. "And I only know of that because one of my wife's relatives, as I already mentioned, enrolled as a novice there. I shall put it to him and see what he comes up with. Drop by again, or telephone, tomorrow morning."

"We shall certainly do so," Mason gratefully replied.

When they got back to their hotel, there was just sufficient time to shower and change before dinner. George Mason was down some time ahead of his young colleague, taking the opportunity of a short stroll along the river embankment and enjoying in solitude - since the detective sergeant disapproved of smoking - one of the Dutch half-coronas he had bought at Ostend. The last of the sight-seeing boats was approaching the quay to unload its complement of tourists, as a pair of four-man sculls, which he took to be university crews in training, raced downstream on the fast current. The twin spires of the Romanesque cathedral, bathed in the glow of the evening sun, seemed to cast a benign eye on a scene disturbed only by the cries of gulls wheeling overhead, light motor traffic and the rumbling of trams along the Limmatquai. As he walked, he mulled over Dieter Lutz's parting suggestion, but try as he might he could not relate the Latin phrase the bookseller had just translated for him to the Potenti in any meaningful way. A motto was fair enough. Lots of institutions, especially schools and colleges, had Latin mottoes. Beyond that, he felt stumped.

Alison was waiting for him in the foyer by the time he returned. They then joined the other guests in the restaurant, occupying a table overlooking the river. The young sergeant was wearing an outfit the detective had not seen before, one that she had retrieved from the suitcase left in the Hauptbahnhof locker. He complimented her on it, to her evident pleasure.

"I wonder if they do raclettes here," she said. "I enjoyed it so much that time we had it at Glarus."

George Mason scanned the menu and shook his head.

"But they do serve cheese fondue," he suggested, "which is rather similar. It is for a minimum of two people, so we could share a dish together, if you wish."

"What exactly is fondue?" Alison wanted to know.

"Basically, it is a bowl of melted cheese," he replied, "cooked in white wine and kirsch, with garlic and nutmeg added. It comes with bread cubes and a long, two-pronged fork for dipping them into the cheese."

"Would that be Swiss cheese?" she asked.

"Absolutely," came the reply. "Emmental and Gruyere, to be precise."

"Sounds appetizing," Alison said. "Let us opt for that, as something typically Swiss."

Mason placed the order, to include a bottle of fondant wine to accompany it, sat back in his chair and casually appraised their fellow-diners. A fondue bowl was being placed over a flame at a nearby table. He drew his companion's attention to it.

"Quite an elaborate little ritual, George," she remarked, "by the look of it."

"They will adjust the flame downward after a while," he explained, "to avoid caking the cheese on the bottom of the bowl."

"But, meanwhile, the heat keeps it nicely molten," she remarked, getting the idea. "I can't wait to try it."

"What was your reaction to Dieter Lutz's input?" he asked, changing tack. "I have been pondering all evening the possible relevance of this new Latin phrase."

Alison returned a sympathetic look, noting that her senior colleague seemed unusually preoccupied.

"I too have given the matter quite a lot of thought," she said, "and you may think this is just wild guesswork."

"Or perhaps feminine intuition?" George Mason gallantly replied. "Whatever it is, don't hold back."

"It occurred to me," the young woman went on, "that if the second part of the quotation represents the Potenti motto, the first part may possibly refer to a website. Presumably, an international society like that will make full use of the internet, for speed of communication. Also for confidentiality."

The detective gave her a long, penetrating look, but did not immediately reply. Behind those candid hazel eyes, he considered, there lurked a keen intelligence. Keen as mustard, in fact. No wonder James Maitland had singled her out for fast-track promotion.

"You know, Alison," he said, admiringly, "your theory may very well be correct."

"We can soon put it to the test," Alison continued. "There is a computer alcove in the hotel main lounge. The staff do not advertise it, probably to deter random use and reserve it for business people and the like, who genuinely need on-line access while traveling."

"So how did you come to learn of it?" he enquired.

"The manager, Herr Staheli, met me in the foyer just now and mentioned it to me. He is aware that we are not regular tourists."

At that point, the fondue arrived, accompanied by the ritual of lighting the table burner. Alison peered into the large bowl, savoring the complex aromas rising from it, while allowing her colleague to take the lead in skewering the first cube of bread to dip in. She quickly followed suit, and for the next half-hour they were content to enjoy their unusual dinner. Fondue being a shared meal, Alison was more than ever pleased that she had switched her main loyalty from the superintendent to George Mason. The latter was a real card, she decided, who knew his way round Europe like it was the Home Counties, and who also knew how to entertain.

"You enjoyed it?" Mason rather superfluously asked, as the table burner finally flickered out.

"Absolutely," came the response. "I shall look up a good recipe when we get back home."

"It is actually quite difficult to make," he warned her. "I

know because I have tried with mixed success on several occasions. I couldn't get the cheese to the correct consistency. It was either too thick or too runny."

"I shall invite you round for a fondue evening," she generously offered, "soon as I have mastered the art."

"I imagine you will, too," he gamely allowed.

When the coffee arrived, they took it with them to the computer alcove, which at this hour was vacant, most of the guests being still at dinner. George Mason sat down at the keyboard, with Alison standing by his side.

"Key in the first part of the quotation," she urged.

The detective did so and, sure enough, the website <www.feci-quod-potui> appeared on the screen, with an instruction to enter the password.

"By Jove, you are right, Alison!" he exclaimed, almost beside himself. "But what do we do now, since we do not know the password?"

"Try Kasimir," Alison hastily suggested.

Mason entered it, but received no reply beyond 'Invalid Password'.

"How about Pliny?"

He did as instructed, but received the same negative response.

"I doubt we shall come up with a password by trial and error," he said, rising from the console and scratching his head.

"Why not ring Dieter Lutz?" Alison suggested. "He is the only reliable resource we have on the ultra-secretive Potenti."

"That is true enough," her colleague agreed. "Why don't you relax here in the lounge and finish your coffee while I try to contact him, assuming of course that he is still at Schipfe?"

With that, George Mason went directly to the phone booth in the foyer, consulted the telephone directory and dialed.

"Dieter Lutz," came the immediate response.

"George Mason again," the detective explained. "I am surprised to find you still at work."

"I was, in fact, on the point of leaving," the antiquarian replied. "The cataloging took longer than I anticipated. What is it that you require, Herr Mason?"

"My colleague and I have managed to discover the Potenti website on our hotel computer, but we cannot access it without a password."

"Sounds reasonable enough," the other replied, "since you are dealing with a secret society. A very secret society, I may add."

"I was wondering if you could come up with some suggestions?" Mason tentatively asked.

Lutz pondered the request for a few moments, before saying:

"I could try to contact the former novice I mentioned. He would be the best bet, having often overheard table talk at the priory. It is a long shot, given the order's secretiveness, but somebody may have slipped something out inadvertently. Give me an hour or so, Herr Mason. I live on Zurichberg, about twenty minutes from here by tram. If I can contact my wife's relative, I shall call you back at your hotel."

"I would be much obliged if you could do that," the detective replied.

"I shall get back to you, one way or the other," the bookseller promised, ringing off.

Mason replaced the receiver and went to join an expectant Alison Aubrey in the spacious lounge, where games of chess or cards were in progress.

"Well, George?" she hopefully enquired.

"Herr Lutz is working on it," he explained. "I managed to catch him just before he left his premises."

"What a stroke of luck!" Alison said.

"He is going to ring me back later on. If you like, we could hang out in the main bar for a while. They have a traditional jazz group billed for this evening."

"Sounds good, George," she remarked, rising from her seat. "I could use a bit of light entertainment after all this arcane stuff about secret societies and Latin mottoes. It fairly makes one's head spin."

*

The following morning, just as the Scotland Yard agents were finishing breakfast, the waiter summoned George Mason to the telephone. Giving his colleague a knowing look, the senior detective rose to his feet and quickly left the dining-room.

"Sorry I did not respond last evening," Dieter Lutz said, apologetically. "It was turned eleven o'clock when I managed to contact the former novice, who had been hiking in the Jura Mountains. I thought you might have retired for the night and did not wish to disturb you."

"Very considerate of you, Herr Lutz," an agreeably surprised George Mason returned. "I thought you might have drawn a blank and chosen not to ring me back."

"Far from it," the bookseller assured him. "Anton Becker, which is the young man's name, does in fact know the password! Which does not altogether surprise me, Herr Mason. He informed me that some selected novices at St.

Kasimir's, the ones considered to be of above-average potential, were given the opportunity of learning about the Diligenti, in case they wished to join when they became fully-fledged monks. Anton was one of the chosen few."

George Mason chuckled to himself at the inner workings of the Potenti, no less than at this sudden turn-up.

"That is great news," he said. "But I do not imagine you are going to reveal the password over the phone."

"Evidently not, Herr Mason," came the reply. "But I can e-mail it to you, if you give me an appropriate address."

"Sounds good."

"But there is one condition," the other explained.

"And what might that be?" Mason guardedly enquired.

"Anton is asking a thousand Swiss francs for the information."

George Mason gasped.

"I can understand that you are a bit taken aback," the antiquarian said. "But you surely appreciate that Anton is taking a considerable risk in divulging such highly-confidential information. If it ever came to light..."

"You mean that they would seek to take revenge?"

"Nothing so drastic as physical harm, Herr Mason. Set your mind at rest on that score. But the Potenti do have sufficient influence in many circles to seriously compromise his career prospects."

"We could not let that happen," the detective said, quickly regaining his equanimity and seeing no alternative to meeting the young man's terms. "But I do not have such a sum of money at short notice."

"A credit card, perhaps?" Lutz prompted. "I could put the payment through my business account and e-mail you the password directly."

Mason fished in his wallet for his Visa and read its

number to the bookseller in addition to supplying his e-mail address. He then returned to the dining-room to finish his meal of liverwurst and scrambled eggs, grown rather cool in the meantime.

"We are in luck, Alison," he remarked, on rejoining her. "But it will cost money."

"Can we afford it?" she asked, with a look of concern.

"We have no other choice," he replied. "I put it on my credit card, to reclaim later. Bill Harrington will have apoplexy, but we cannot help that." He nudged the remains of his meal aside, saying: "Finish your coffee and we shall pay another visit to the hotel computer."

Seated at the console minutes later, they opened a message from Dieter Lutz. It contained only the password and nothing more.

"Sicilianvespers!" Mason exclaimed. "That is a clear nod to the Vespertines, if ever there was one. Let us key it in at once to their website, <feci-quod-potui>."

Moments later, the two detectives broached the secret world of the Potenti, something they would never have achieved had not a certain Leonard Parks fallen from a tourist boat on the Danube. The society's general aims and philosophy were set out in some detail, as was its historical connection to the Illuminati - the Enlightened Ones - of eighteenth-century Bavaria. The junior branch of Diligenti was also described, its function being to materially assist the Potenti in a range of practical ways. Members of both cadres were sworn to absolute secrecy.

"What do you make of all this, Alison?" he excitedly enquired.

"Quite fascinating," she replied, without mentioning that Superintendent Maitland's e-mail address began with the letters fqp.

"I surmised some days ago, while talking to Dieter Lutz," George Mason then said, "that their objective could be to infiltrate government circles. According to this website, that was to be only the start. They apparently also have their sights on the International Monetary Fund!"

"To achieve a global reach, no less," Alison remarked.

"It would appear so, Alison. Their immediate aim, however, seems to be to corner for one of their members a key post at the European Commission in Brussels, using calculated bribes for the purpose."

"Slush funds, George?"

"Exactly," came the reply. "But they do not give details of their sources, only to commend Professor Paul Jarvis for his success in fund-raising."

"So you were right to be concerned about Leonard Parks being in the care of the Vespertines," Alison remarked. "They would have to make doubly sure he did not expose Professor Jarvis at this critical juncture in their scheme. His amnesia must have been a God-send to them."

George Mason continued his perusal of the website, to glean as much as he could about the inner workings of the secret society. Eventually, he said:

"You are certainly right about that, Alison. We shall inform Superintendent Maitland of our findings soon as we get back to London."

"I would not do that, if I were you, George," she advised. "I would go higher up, to the very top. To the Police Commissioner himself, Sir Giles Pettigrew."

"Perhaps you are right," he replied, surprised that she would by-pass the very person who had assigned her to this mission. On reflection, it suited him. Maitland had gotten rather too big for his boots of late, probably angling for a knighthood in the New Year honors list.

Alison smiled to herself at his ready acquiescence. George Mason, she knew, would just love to learn about her suspicions of the superintendent. She had grown aware in the course of this long trip that there was no love lost between the two men; yet she needed hard evidence to name James Maitland as a possible co-conspirator in what was beginning to look like a case of high political intrigue.

"Doesn't the website list the membership?" she asked him.

"Apparently not," her puzzled colleague replied. "All it gives here, apart from general aims, philosophy and history, is the name of a business company registered in Bermuda, at 1103 Atlantic Parade, Hamilton."

The young sergeant peered over his shoulder.

"Tewkesbury Holdings?" she asked.

"That is what it says here," George Mason said. "When we reach London, we shall check it out at Companies House on The Strand and find out who the directors are. I would stake half my pension they include key players in the Potenti."

"My head is swimming with all this," Alison ruefully complained. "I need some fresh air."

George Mason took the hint and immediately logged off, glancing up sympathetically at his young colleague and rising from the console. A fine morning greeted them as they shortly afterwards stepped outdoors, noting that the river boats were beginning to load up with groups of eager tourists. They strolled along the Limmat embankment to the Hauptbahnhof, so that Mason could obtain a copy of the London *Times* from the bookstall. Alison Aubrey took the opportunity to do some personal shopping at the various boutiques lining the station concourse, while her less-active colleague ordered fresh coffee in the cafeteria and caught up with the news from England. When they eventually got back to their hotel, there was a message waiting for them to contact Dieter Lutz without delay.

CHAPTER TWELVE

In the early afternoon, after a quick lunch, the two detectives made their way along Bahnhofstrasse to the embarkation point for passengers to Rapperswil, situated at the eastern end of Lake Zurich. A telephone conversation with Dieter Lutz had drawn the information, via Anton Becker, that the Vespertines operated, in tandem with an obscure order of nuns, a rehabilitation center for drug addicts and alcoholics in the lakeside town. Becker did not know, however, if the center offered a broader spectrum of medical treatments, to include cures for amnesia. That did not surprise George Mason. There was a certain irony, he felt, in the fact that Leonard Parks, having been found inebriated, should have ended up in a facility for alcoholics, if indeed that was his present location. Anticipating possible resistance on the parts of the center's staff, he had taken the step of alerting Leutnant Rudi Kubler of the Zurich Polizei Dienst. Kubler was tied up until noon, and had suggested that the Scotland Yard agents go ahead by boat. He himself would drive down to Rapperswil the minute he was free and meet them there.

It was a fine day for a sail. Having bought tickets at the quayside kiosk, they sat on the foredeck and waited patiently for the *Uri* to ease away from the dock. Holding a course down the center of the lake, it offered clear views of either bank. On the northern side were mainly luxury hotels and office buildings; on the southern, the manicured gardens of suburban villas reached down to the water's edge, some with yachts at private moorings. The good life, Mason reflected with a tinge of envy, as enjoyed by film stars, financiers, sports personalities and the like. His companion's eye, meanwhile, was drawn to the bathing station and the broad park on the northern shore, which were frequented mainly by the younger element of Zurich society. As they journeyed east, the snow-capped alps loomed ever larger, seeming almost to close in on them as the vessel eventually berthed at Rapperswil. Leutnant Kubler was sitting on a bench beneath a row of chestnut trees, perusing a batch of police reports as he waited.

"My meeting ended early," he explained, as he rose to greet them. "I have been sitting here for the past fifteen minutes watching your boat approach. Did you enjoy the trip?"

"It was wonderful," Alison remarked. "I had no idea Lake Zurich was so large and the scenery so varied."

"It is about thirty miles long," the Swiss officer said. "Even so, it is one of the smaller lakes in Switzerland."

"All we have to do now," George Mason said, glancing round appreciatively at the picturesque town and its mellow stone buildings, "is to locate Kurcentrum Rapperswil."

"It is just along there," Kubler informed them, with a wave of his arm, "in the lee of the castle walls."

The trio proceeded to the far end of the quay, crossed the street and approached a large mansion set in its own grounds. A young nun, clad in a light-blue habit and white wimple, who was tending to patients sunning themselves on recliners in the front garden, interrupted her ministrations and confronted them.

"We wish to speak with your director," Leutnant Kubler stated in German, lending the full weight of his office to his request.

The nun made no verbal reply, simply bowing slightly before leading the way indoors as far as a small office at the end of the short corridor. She rapped on the frosted-glass window, waited a moment, then silently withdrew.

"*Hinein!*" came a call from within.

The trio entered as the occupant, clad in a darker habit than the first nun, rose from behind her desk on spotting a uniformed officer and stepped apprehensively towards them.

"Mother Elfriede," she said, introducing herself, "of the Sisters of Serenity. I am the directress of the Kurcentrum. What is your business here?"

Rudi Kubler turned towards George Mason, who produced the photograph of the missing tax inspector he had obtained from Milos Foldes.

"We have reason to believe, madam," Kubler explained, "that the individual shown in this photograph may be staying at your facility."

The nun took the picture and peered at it closely, her eyes soon lighting up in recognition.

"Indeed, he is in residence here," she said, "in our rehabilitation program for alcoholics."

"What name is he registered under?" George Mason asked, in his best German.

"Unfortunately," came the reply, "he cannot tell us who he is, since he appears to be also suffering from amnesia."

"How long has he been in your care, Mother Elfriede?" the detective continued.

"For a few weeks," came the quick reply. "He was

brought to us by three Vespertine monks, who informed me that he had some connection with their order."

"Are those two monks attached to this facility?" Leutnant Kubler asked.

The nun emphatically shook her head.

"We do have Vespertines here," she explained, "to assist with the more aggressive male patients, but they are not the same ones who brought the person in this photograph."

"Would it be possible to speak with them?" Mason asked.

"Unfortunately not," the directress replied. "They are away all this week on a retreat at their priory at Glarus."

George Mason and Alison Aubrey smiled to each other at this confirmation of the connection with St. Kasimir's.

"We have reason to believe," Kubler then said, "that this patient was abducted from a hospital at Vacs, Hungary. This gentleman here and his assistant are detectives from Metropolitan Police headquarters in London. They have been trying to trace him since he was reported missing by his wife, who lives in northern England. By dint of thorough investigation, and a little bit of luck, the trail has led them here, to Kurcentrum Rapperswil. They requested that I accompany them."

The face of the nun registered shock and disbelief.

"This cannot possibly be true," she protested. "I am sure that the monks would only act in the best of faith."

"Nevertheless, Reverend Mother," Kubler said, "we are obliged to treat it as an abduction and are transferring the nameless patient into our care. Please lead us to him at once."

"Then follow me, Leutnant," the nun curtly replied, leading them towards the rear of the building. "But I am sure there will be serious repercussions. The Vespertines

188

are very influential in these parts, on account of their charitable works."

"There can be little doubt about that," George Mason said, in an aside to Alison Aubrey, as they entered a small rear garden enclosed by ivy-covered walls.

"I shall take full responsibility for any fall-out," Kubler said, to allay the nun's misgivings, as she strode up to a man sitting under a large birch-tree, engrossed in a newspaper. He looked exactly like his image in the photograph, except that his features seemed a little drawn and his complexion paler. Lingering effects, Mason surmised, of his misadventure on the Danube River.

He rose at their approach, presenting a somewhat taller, ganglier figure than the detective had imagined, his tousled hair falling across his forehead and a vague, questioning look in his dark eyes.

"Leonard Parks?" George Mason asked, extending his right hand.

The man returned a look of puzzlement, but willingly shook hands. Smiling weakly, he said in slightly-accented English:

"Fine day, isn't it?"

"Indeed it is," Alison Aubrey responded, hoping that the sound of an Englishwoman's voice might prompt recollection of his wife, Justine.

"These people are here to help you," Mother Elfriede then said, now seemingly resigned to the situation. "Gather your few belongings together and report to my office, where I shall authorize your release. The Sisters of Serenity will then have no further responsibility for your welfare."

"Where are you taking me?" the patient warily enquired.

"We shall provide you with first-rate care," George Mason assured him, "to ensure your full recovery. We shall also contact your wife, Justine."

Mention of Justine produced no visible effect whatsoever. Leonard Parks went up to his room and soon returned with his few belongings. The brief formalities completed, they bade good-bye to the directress, left the building and strode towards the lieutenant's parked car for the return drive to Zurich.

"Where now?" an intrigued George Mason asked his Swiss counterpart.

"To Weselius Klinik," Kubler replied. "It is close to the lake, on the eastern outskirts of the city. Carl Gustav Jung, the eminent psychiatrist, had connections with it. It boasts some of the highest-qualified physicians in Switzerland."

"I have a feeling we are going to need them," Alison Aubrey wryly remarked.

*

Later that same day, Superintendent James Maitland received a telephone call from Glarus, as a result of which he placed an urgent call to Sir Maurice Weeks at the Exchequer. The latter was in conference with the Prime Minister. It was almost an hour later, approaching five o'clock, when he returned the call.

"What is the problem, Jim?" he brusquely enquired, keen to be on his way home ahead of the rush-hour traffic.

"Serious developments in Switzerland," Maitland replied. "Leonard Parks has been sprung from Kurcentrum Rapperswil!"

"By whom?" asked the astonished First Secretary.

"By Inspector George Mason of Scotland Yard and a Zurich police lieutenant named Rudi Kubler."

The senior civil servant verged on apoplexy.

"I understood that you were going to give that confounded Mason firm instructions to return to London!" he barked.

"I have been waiting several days for Detective Sergeant Aubrey to phone in her latest report," the superintendent timorously explained. "But, for reasons beyond me, she has failed to do so. I have no idea what is going on across the English Channel."

"Then you had better make it your business to find out, Jim," Weeks returned. "What if Parks decides to talk?"

"Hardly likely, Sir Maurice, since he is suffering from amnesia. Apparently, he still does not even know his own name, according to the medical personnel employed at the clinic."

Sir Maurice Weeks thought hard for a few moments.

"All the same," he said, more evenly, "it would be wise to effect damage control. According to your previous report from Alison Aubrey, Parks has already interviewed Professor Jarvis at Zell University, and may therefore be well-aware of his off-shore financial arrangements."

"That is certainly a possibility," Maitland replied. "But it does not necessarily mean that he linked Jarvis with our society, especially since the Diligenti and the Potenti are self-contained, virtually watertight branches of the Illuminati."

The civil servant merely grunted at that.

"That may well be," he said, "but to be on the safe side, instruct Professor Jarvis to close the Cayman account and transfer the funds to Tewkesbury Holdings in Bermuda. That should close off one possible line of enquiry."

"Inspector Mason could not possibly know any more than Leonard Parks chooses to tell him, if and when he recovers his memory," Maitland said. "And, don't forget, as a member of the Diligenti Leonard Parks made a vow of secrecy."

"You have a point there, Superintendent," came the reply. "If at some future date Parks does recover, which now seems more likely since he is out of our hands, and he opts to pursue Jarvis for tax evasion, he may do so. I shall use my influence at Whitehall to help the professor come to a discreet arrangement with the Comptroller of Taxes, to avoid any adverse publicity. Jarvis will make enough from future book royalties and the lecture circuit to make regular payments on what he owes in back taxes. The comptroller should go for that, at my urging, if I mention the public interest."

"Then we can put our minds at rest," the police official said, "clearing the way for our nominee to be appointed Finance Commissioner at Brussels."

"Only when those two detectives are back across the English Channel," Weeks dryly remarked, "will my mind be completely at rest. Alison Aubrey is a comparative rookie at this sort of thing, but Mason's record is well-known even here at the Exchequer. In fact, it is almost legendary."

*

Over dinner that evening, George Mason and Alison Aubrey reviewed the day's events, having earlier helped Leonard Parks check into Weselius Klinik, assuring him of regular visits.

"You must be feeling very pleased with yourself, George," Alison remarked, while enjoying the tiramisu she had ordered for dessert, "now that you have achieved your main objective."

George Mason, having skipped dessert, sipped his liqueur-coffee thoughtfully, half smiled and said:

"So far, so good, Alison. But I have the feeling there is a lot more to unravel about this matter than simply locating Leonard Parks, although nobody will be more pleased about current developments than his wife Justine."

The young officer nudged her empty plate aside, with a sigh of satisfaction.

"I just love tiramisu," she remarked, adding cream to her coffee.

"It is Italian for 'pick-me-up'," Mason knowledgably explained. "Almost as universal as pizza."

"You are really good at languages, aren't you?" she said, admiringly. "I was impressed with your German earlier, at the Rapperswil facility."

"One picks up the odd phrase, here and there," he casually replied. "It is a hobby of mine, sort of, and very useful on assignments like this. But listen carefully, Alison. I think our best move now is for you to return to London, as early as tomorrow in fact. I want you to go to Companies House on The Strand and find out all you can about Tewkesbury Holdings, especially the names of the directors. I think that by doing so we shall discover the names of some key players in the Potenti."

Alison Aubrey was a bit taken aback, but saw the logic of his proposal.

"What do you intend to do, meanwhile?" she asked.

"In the short term, I intend to stay in touch with Leonard Parks," he replied, "and monitor his progress. Whatever you find out in London, keep under your hat until I return. Do not tell a soul."

Alison immediately thought of James Maitland, but did not mention his name to her colleague. She also realized that she would have to come up with a convincing explanation on reaching London for failing to ring the superintendent. It was something she would figure out on the return flight from Kloten Airport.

"If you have finished your meal," Mason then said, "I suggest you go up to your room and pack your luggage in readiness for an early departure tomorrow morning. Meet me in the bar later for a nightcap, if you feel inclined."

Back in his own room, he placed a telephone call to Balderstones.

"Good news a last, Justine!" he said, as the line became live.

"You have found Leonard!" she exclaimed, with a sigh of intense relief. "How is he, Inspector Mason?"

"Safe and well," the detective replied. "But there is a problem, I am afraid."

"What exactly do you mean by that?" Justine warily enquired.

"Your husband had an unfortunate accident in Hungary," the detective explained, "as a result of which he seems to have lost his memory. That could explain why he has not contacted you in all this time."

"How dreadful," came the concerned reply. "What sort of accident, Inspector?"

George Mason was careful to put the most positive spin on the incident, even though in his own mind there remained the possibility that her husband had made an attempt on his own life.

"He went overboard from a Danube riverboat," he told her, "and apparently struck his head on something in the water, probably a piece of flotsam. By a stroke of luck, the crew of a passing barge rescued him and took him to the hospital at a town called Vacs, near the border with

Austria."

It took a while for the news to sink in.

"This is all very confusing," Justine eventually said. "Had Leonard been drinking, by any chance?"

"He had had one or two, I believe," Mason diplomatically replied, "according to his old college friend, Milos Foldes."

"That sounds plausible, Inspector," Justine remarked. "Leonard does tend to drink heavily when under stress. Where exactly are you calling from?"

"From my hotel in Zurich," the detective replied. "Leonard is being treated at a well-known clinic here. His physician, Dr. Weingarten, is reasonably confident he will recover his memory. The question is when."

"Is there anything I can do to help?" Justine asked. "I simply cannot get away from here at the present. The new term has barely begun at the village school."

"Dr. Weingarten suggested you send things that might help jog his memory. Family photographs, favorite CDs, books. Anything of that sort, in fact."

"I shall see to it straight away," she replied. "He will particularly appreciate a recording of Bartok, who came from the same region of Hungary. I shall mail him his CD of *Bluebeard's Castle*, with copies of our wedding photographs and two of his books."

"That should help a lot," George Mason agreed.

"And you should contact his mother, Léni," Justine added, "as soon as possible. Bring her to see him at the clinic."

"That can easily be arranged," he assured her.

"And please ring me whenever you can, Inspector, to report on Leonard's progress. If he is still under treatment by half-term, I shall make arrangements to come to Zurich.

I trust you implicitly, to make sure he receives good care."

"Hopefully, we shall have him back in England well before then," George Mason said, pleased at her vote of confidence.

Replacing the receiver, he dialed the Oerlikon number for Léni Farkas, but got no answer. He thought that was a bit odd, since she seemed to him largely house-bound. He would try again later from the hotel foyer, he decided, before taking his nightcap in the bar. The detective sergeant did not join him; he presumed she had retired early.

*

When Alison Aubrey arrived at Scotland Yard on the day following her return flight from Zurich, she was informed by Chief Inspector Harrington that James Maitland was tied up with urgent business for the next several days and was to be left undisturbed. The news came as a relief to the young sergeant, who had been racking her brains on the way over for a plausible explanation of her failure to continue making regular telephone reports from the Continent.

"Now tell me, Sergeant Aubrey, what you and Inspector Mason have managed to come up with in all this time," Harrington testily remarked.

"We located Leonard Parks," she proudly announced. "George Mason is staying close to him in Zurich, where he is undergoing treatment for amnesia."

"Parks has been wandering round Europe all this time, not even knowing who he is?" an astonished Bill Harrington asked.

"Something along those lines, Chief Inspector," the young detective replied, smiling to herself at his turn of phrase.

"The Government will be delighted you have found him. I shall inform Sir Maurice Weeks at once."

"I would not do so just yet," Alison cautioned.

"Why ever not, Sergeant?"

"George Mason thinks there may be ramifications to the Parks case that require further investigation. I should wait, if you are willing, until he gets back to England."

Bill Harrington poured himself a tot of Glen Garioch single-malt whisky to chase his morning coffee, sipped it thoughtfully and peered closely at the young officer before deciding to give her the benefit of the doubt.

"This is most irregular," he replied, after a while, "but if Mason has something up his sleeve, I am prepared to hold fire for the time being, at least until the superintendent is available. This is really James Maitland's province, in any case."

Alison Aubrey smiled in gratitude.

"My hunch is that you will not regret your decision," she remarked.

On eventually leaving Scotland Yard, she crossed to Westminster Underground and took the Circle Line to Charing Cross. A short walk up The Strand in the direction of Fleet Street brought her to Companies House, where she researched the list of British companies registered in Bermuda. There was, however, no record of a company named Tewkesbury Holdings, which caused her both surprise and puzzlement, since it had featured prominently on the Potenti website. Not too familiar with commercial procedures and company matters, she approached the enquiry desk and asked to speak to an official. Within minutes, an elderly gentleman in a black jacket and pin-stripe trousers greeted her and invited her into an interview room.

"How can I be of assistance to you?" he helpfully enquired.

"I have been trying to obtain public information on a company called Tewkesbury Holdings," she replied. "It is supposedly registered in Hamilton, Bermuda."

The official noted the name and disappeared for a while, promising to look into the matter, leaving the visitor to admire the paintings on the walls, mainly scenes of the South Downs and the Sussex coast. Fifteen minutes later, he returned.

"There is no business entity of that name listed here at Companies House," he informed her.

"What would that imply?" Alison asked him.

The official returned a faintly ironic smile and said:

"One possibility is that it is a shell company."

"What exactly do you mean by that?"

"It could be a front for money laundering, tax evasion, drug receipts or any other form of illicit gains," the official explained.

"Would such a company have directors and other personnel?" she asked.

"It could well have," came the considered reply. "But their names would not be publicly disclosed."

"So there would be no way of finding out who they are?"

"The only way you could do that," the official explained, "is to go to the Metropolitan Police and have them request the Bermuda police to check the island's banks for an account in the name of Tewkesbury Holdings. If the company does have directors, they will presumably be signatories to that account, so that they can draw on it as circumstances dictate. In fact, if you suspect malfeasance, it would be your civic duty to report it to the authorities. May

I enquire the nature of your interest in this matter?"

"I am a police officer, my good sir, based at Scotland Yard," the detective sergeant replied, noting with a smile the man's surprised reaction. "I appreciate your advice and shall certainly act upon it."

"Only too glad to be of assistance, madam," the official said, in more deferential tones, "if it helps in the fight against crime."

How fortuitous, Alison Aubrey considered as she strolled back along The Strand, that Superintendent Maitland was currently tied up on other matters. She could ask Bill Harrington to make the necessary approach to the authorities in Bermuda, without alerting the Potenti and putting them on their guard. She strongly suspected, from the style of his e-mail address, that James Maitland was a member of that society. As she entered Charing Cross Underground and rode down the escalator to the Circle Line platform, she felt a sudden frisson of excitement. This was top detective work, she mused, far more interesting than burglaries, traffic violations and the whole gamut of run-of-the-mill crimes and misdemeanors. And who could tell what may come to light at the end of the day?

CHAPTER THIRTEEN

After two weeks' residence at Weselius Klinik, a significant breakthrough in Leonard Parks' treatment occurred. Dr. Weingarten, the clinical psychologist, had diagnosed retrograde amnesia and had instituted a regime of individual and group therapy. The family photographs, CDs and memorabilia Justine had sent helped a lot. George Mason had also visited most days talking about various aspects of life in England, while trying to jog the patient's memory about the itinerary they had each recently followed across half of Europe. Towards the end of the second week, the detective had at last succeeded in contacting Léni Farkas, who had been in hospital for a hip replacement. Her appearance at the clinic on the Friday morning proved to be the clincher. Leonard Parks recognized her within minutes and things went rapidly uphill from there.

"Anya!" the patient exclaimed, using the Hungarian for mother. "Delighted to see you!"

"Not nearly so pleased as I am," the aristocratic old lady replied, "to find you looking fit and well after your long ordeal."

"I have had excellent care," her son said, "by Dr. Weingarten and his staff. But I do not understand what all the fuss is about."

"You have only been missing for several weeks," Léni informed him. "Have you any recollection of your movements since you left my apartment and went to visit your father, the count's grave at Glarus?"

Leonard Parks, guiding the frail woman to an easy chair, gave some thought to her question, but was slow in replying.

"It is starting to come back to me now, very slowly," he said, after a while. "I do recall visiting the grave and placing fresh flowers on it, as well as meeting briefly with the prior, Fr. Dominic. After that, I took the train to Innsbruck."

"Did you call at a stamp dealer's there?" George Mason asked him.

"Gertweiler's," came the surprised response. "I called on them to complete my set of military stamps of the Third Reich. How could you know something like that, Inspector Mason?"

"Their telephone number is listed in your diary," the detective replied, reaching inside his jacket pocket and handing it to him. "You mislaid it at Hotel Adler, Zurich. The manager, Herr Staheli, aware that I was looking for you, entrusted it to me for safe-keeping."

"Leonard was always a keen stamp collector," Léni Farkas remarked, "like his father before him."

"After Innsbruck, where did you go next?" the detective asked.

A pained expression crossed the patient's face, as if recalling something unpleasant.

"I went to Zell, in the Austrian Tyrol," he replied, in a low voice. "Let us not talk about that."

"Very well," George Mason agreed. "Where did you go after leaving Zell?"

Leonard Parks' face lit up in a broad smile.

"I went to visit my old college friend, Milos Foldes, at Budapest," he replied. "After that, I have no recollection whatsoever."

Mason was not too surprised on hearing that. Dr. Weingarten had warned him that certain events, particularly traumatic ones, could remain permanently buried in the patient's subconscious.

"Do you recall taking a boat trip on the Danube, as far as Visegrad?" he prompted.

The patient shook his head, decisively.

"I have no recollection of that," he said, "nor of much else, until I came to at the hospital in Vacs."

"Why are you asking him all these questions, Inspector Mason?" a concerned Leni Farkas asked.

"There are certain facts I need to establish, Madam," the detective explained, "to get as complete a picture as possible."

"There is surely no hurry, Inspector," Leni said. "Why not come back tomorrow and let me and my son enjoy this first day together after such a long and painful separation. This afternoon, he must also call Justine as soon as she arrives home from school."

George Mason took the none-too-subtle hint and tactfully withdrew. Quitting the clinic, he strolled back towards the city center along the strand, enjoying the fresh breeze blowing across the lake. After a while, he stopped off at a garden restaurant for a beer and a grilled bratwurst, wondering as he watched the yachts tacking across the water how Alison Aubrey was faring in London. He was assuming that she had already been to Companies House on the errand he had assigned her. But why, he asked himself, had she not contacted him in all this time? The uneasy thought crossed his mind that James Maitland might have something to do with that. As the superintendent's protégé, she may have decided that her first loyalty was to him.

His misgivings on that score were allayed, however, as soon as he got back to his hotel. There was an envelope with British postage waiting for him at Reception. He took it to the lounge facing the river, opened it and perused the contents. It was from the detective sergeant. She began with a wordy account of her visit to Companies House on The Strand, her subsequent meeting with Bill Harrington and their liaison with the Bermuda police. Then she gave names. Far from switching her loyalty to Superintendent Maitland, as he had feared, she was in fact naming that very person as one of the directors of a shell company known as Tewkesbury Holdings!

When he had recovered from his initial shock, he read the other names. Incredibly, they included Sir Maurice Weeks, First Secretary at the Exchequer. Less surprising was the name of Professor Paul Jarvis. There followed a string of Europeans who meant little to him personally, yet they were evidently significant figures in their home countries, all key members of the secret society known as the Potenti: Aristide Lebrun, a Parisian lawyer; Pasquale Viti, chairman of Banca Popolare; Volker Schmidt, a prominent German industrialist, and a half-dozen others. Her letter ended with a request for him to telephone her to keep abreast of further developments. Replacing the letter in the envelope, he went up to his room and placed a call to her home at Henley-on-Thames.

"I just got your letter, Alison," he said, as the line became live.

"Interesting reading, don't you think, George?" she remarked.

"Very much so," he replied. "Whoever would have suspected James Maitland and Sir Maurice Weeks, of all people, to be members of an international conspiracy?"

"I have had a nagging suspicion about Superintendent Maitland," Alison replied, "since part-way through our investigation."

"Have you, indeed, Alison?" her colleague replied. "You kept very quiet about it." There was a hint almost of reproach in his voice.

"I did not mention it," she said, sensing his pique, "because it seemed so improbable. I needed confirmation."

"So what happens next?" Mason asked. "You are evidently several steps ahead of me."

"Chief Inspector Harrington and I met yesterday with the Police Commissioner, Sir Giles Pettigrew. We showed him the names we had obtained from Bermuda. He was astounded, of course, especially to see the First Secretary and the Superintendent listed."

"You managed to avoid a run-in with Maitland?"

"He has been away from London, by a stroke of luck, these last several days," Alison said. "First thing Monday morning, when he is due to return to Whitehall, Sir Giles will confront him with charges of political subversion, conspiracy and bribery. Sir Maurice Weeks has already been challenged and is consulting his lawyers. Information has been sent via Europol to various European authorities, naming the other individuals involved. The Prime Minister and the President of the European Commission have also been informed."

"That should hamstring the Potenti for quite some time to come," George Mason observed, with satisfaction.

"If it does not neuter them for good," the young sergeant replied.

"I would not count very heavily on that, Alison," Mason remarked. "A secretive organization like the Potenti will have depths of resilience and resources that may never fully come to light. After all, they have been around, even if below the radar, since before the French Revolution. Their immediate objectives may be stymied and key figures may do jail-time, but they will regroup eventually and find new agendas."

"I expect you are right about that, George," Alison reluctantly conceded, switching the subject to Leonard Parks.

"He is doing quite nicely, surprisingly," Mason informed her, "thanks to expert psychiatric care. He has recovered most of his memory, except for events between Budapest and Vacs, which remain a complete blank. I shall be flying back to England with him on Sunday, to reunite him with his wife."

"You will be in good time to get in on the act, George, when they charge Weeks and Maitland. It will be a media spectacle."

"You bet, Alison! The political scandal of the decade, I shouldn't wonder. I am looking forward to it. And thanks for the sterling part you played in solving the mystery. I do not know what I would have done without you."

"I think the honors are just about even," Alison replied. "You discovered the meaning of the Latin quotation from Dieter Lutz; whereas I came to realize that the initial letters of *feci quod potui* – fpq, in fact - formed part of Superintendent Maitland's e-mail address."

"Which is why you did not want me to contact the superintendent immediately after we accessed the Potenti website?" Mason said. "You had already had your suspicions about him."

"I could not reveal any of my thinking, even to you George, before visiting Companies House," she explained. "I needed tangible proof. That was provided by the Bermuda authorities, in the form of signatories to a bank account on the island. Tewkesbury Holdings is a front company for the Potenti."

"You did the right thing, Alison," he complimented, before ringing off and grabbing a towel to take down to the hotel sauna. First, he mixed himself a whisky-and-soda from the mini-bar, to celebrate.

*

On the Saturday morning, George Mason made his way to Weselius Klinik looking forward, as he walked briskly along the lakeside promenade, to his next interview with Leonard Parks, who had spent most of the previous day catching up with family. Mason found him in good spirits, watching television by himself in the patients' lounge.

"Good to see you looking so well," the detective remarked, occupying a chair close by him.

"No small thanks to you, Inspector," the other replied, with a broad smile. "I spoke with Justine last evening. She too is extremely grateful for all you have done. Dr. Weingarten will discharge me first thing after breakfast tomorrow morning. We can both return home."

"What was his final diagnosis?" Mason asked.

"Temporary amnesia due to high alcohol intake," Parks ruefully replied, "aggravated by a heavy blow on the head."

"You do not recall going overboard?"

"I have no recollection at all of what happened after I left Budapest."

"Your friend Milos told me you had been drinking rather

heavily."

"That is true," Parks admitted. "I had a great deal on my mind at the time."

"Occasioned by your visit to a certain Professor Paul Jarvis?"

The Inland Revenue agent returned a look of astonishment.

"How could you possibly know something like that?" he queried.

"Would I be correct in saying that you suffered a severe conflict of loyalties?" Mason asked, side-stepping his question.

"You really do amaze me, Inspector Mason," Parks said. "That, precisely, was the root of the problem."

"Occasioned when you noticed the Potenti coat-of-arms on the desk of the professor's study at Zell University?"

Leonard Parks abruptly stood up and paced the lounge, agitatedly.

"You are not going to tell me," he said, on regaining his composure, "that you are familiar with the Potenti?"

"I must admit to knowing a fair amount about them," the detective replied. "I am also aware that you are a member of their junior branch, the Diligenti."

"You could not possibly know that," the other remonstrated.

"*Faciant meliora potentes*?"

Parks looked so stunned on hearing the Potenti motto that Mason began to fear he might suffer a relapse. After a lengthy silence, however, the beginnings of a smile crossed the taxman's features.

"You really have been doing your homework, Inspector," he generously allowed.

"Do you want to tell me the whole story now?" the

detective gently prodded.

Leonard Parks cleared his throat and said:

"I did, in fact, identify Paul Jarvis as a member of our society from the small shield on his study desk. That immediately presented a conflict, since members of our society are sworn to secrecy and mutual loyalty. But I also had a duty to my employers, the Inland Revenue, to pursue him for tax evasion. This series of investigations, beginning with a person named Colin Sutton at Ostend, and continuing through Zurich and Zell, was very significant for my career prospects. I also felt I had a duty to my wife, Justine, who wants to quit full-time teaching and start a family."

"And that conflict of loyalties was the cause of your bout of heavy drinking?"

Parks gave a heavy sigh, sat down again and nodded in agreement.

"I could not see my way forward," he explained. "And that is not all. There was an additional level of conflict."

"You poor guy," George Mason sympathetically remarked. "You really have been through the mill, haven't you?"

"You can say that again!"

"Do you want to tell me about it?"

"Why not?" the other replied. "If you have penetrated the Potenti, Inspector Mason, an achievement which truly amazes me, you might as well know everything."

"I am all ears," Mason said.

Leonard Parks stood up again, crossed to the far side of the room to the dispenser and returned with two cups of chilled Evian water. At that point, one of the staff nurses briefly appeared to check that everything was in order. She adjusted the Venetian blinds against the glare of the morning sun and tactfully withdrew.

"As I approached the professor's study door, which was partly open," Parks continued, "I overheard him discussing financial matters on the telephone."

"Would that involve a large sum of money?" the detective pointedly asked.

Leonard Parks gaped back at him, in disbelief.

"You really are a most remarkable man, Inspector," he observed.

"Please go on," Mason urged, anxious to hear the rest.

"That telephone conversation did not mean a great deal to me until I read in a newspaper I bought at Innsbruck that a university student by the name of Alena Hruska had been kidnapped and that a large ransom had been demanded of her father, a prominent Czech brewer."

"So you put two and two together?" the detective prompted.

Leonard parks nodded.

"It caused me even more conflict," he explained. "Whether to maintain my loyalty to the society, or go to the police and report a serious crime."

"That would have called for another few drinks, at least," Mason wryly commented.

"I am afraid so," the other admitted, appreciating the other's sense of humor.

"I am going to have to pass on what you have just told me to Leutnant Rudi Kubler of the Zurich police," Mason then said. "He in turn will inform the Austrian authorities, who will arrest Jarvis. Several other arrests of key Potenti members will take place next week in London, Paris and Rome, on charges of political subversion, money laundering, conspiracy and bribery."

The Revenue agent's expression saddened as he sipped

his mineral water.

"I am genuinely sorry to hear that," he remarked. "But I think my days in the society are now numbered. They would expel me in any case, after all this fiasco."

"What made you join them in the first place, Leonard?" George Mason was curious to learn.

"My father, Count Farkas, was a member of the Potenti, as was his father before him. He urged me to carry on the family tradition. I did not wish to make such a strong commitment, so I mollified him by agreeing to join the lower order of the Diligenti."

"*Semper diligens*?"

Leonard Parks returned an ironic smile, saying:

"You seem to know just about everything, Inspector. But do you know how one member of the Diligenti recognizes another?"

His visitor slowly shook his head.

"They cross the first and second fingers of their left hand."

"I thought that was just a sign of good luck," a mystified George Mason said.

"For the most part," the other explained, "that is what it has become in the passage of time. But were you aware that it originated during the Roman Empire? It was the secret way Christians recognized each other during persecutions of the early church. Crossed fingers represented the cross of Christ."

"How fascinating is that!" the detective declared. "Tell me, how exactly do the Diligenti fit into the scheme of things?"

"They operate mainly as a support group," came the reply. "Assisting with logistics, fund-raising and routine administrative tasks. I was also persuaded as a young man that we could help hasten the fall of Communism throughout Eastern Europe, particularly in my native Hungary."

"Which you may well have done," the detective agreed, "since the Potenti credo is the polar opposite to Marxist ideology."

"It was an extra incentive to join," Parks said, "for idealistic university students hoping to promote the good society. It is truly distressing to me to learn that they are now on the wrong side of the law."

"There will be questions about this in the House of Commons," Mason said. "And if, on the outing of Sir Maurice Weeks, First Secretary at the Exchequer, there is a vote of no confidence in the government, the prime minister will need to resign and call a general election."

"Is it as serious as that, Inspector?" the other asked, awed at the prospect.

"You bet," the detective replied, picturing to himself the expression on James Maitland's face when challenged at Scotland Yard on Monday morning.

"Tell me one more thing before you go, Inspector," the recovering amnesiac said.

"If I can, Mr. Parks, certainly."

"You could not possibly have become aware of the Potenti website unless a member of the society had revealed it to you."

"That is absolutely correct," George Mason admitted.

"May I ask who that person was?"

"It was none other than you yourself, Leonard," the detective replied, to his hearer's utter astonishment. "You kept repeating the words *Feci quod potui* in your delirium at Vacs Hospital, after being fished out of the Danube. We figured that those few Latin words held considerable significance for you, so we keyed them into the computer at Hotel Adler in Zurich, on the off-chance. We came up trumps."

The light of understanding spread across Parks' still rather strained features.

"But the secret password?" he queried. "How could you possibly have discovered that?"

"Your Inland Revenue client, Dieter Lutz," George Mason explained, "was very helpful in that regard, as he has been almost from the very outset of this investigation. As well as identifying the author of the Latin quotation as Pliny the Elder, and translating it for me, he also had a useful link to the Vespertines."

Leonard Parks returned a wry smile, as it dawned on him that some individual had evidently broken the vow of *Omerta*, the oath of silence enjoined on all members of the society.

"A stroke of luck for you, Inspector," he simply remarked, "that one of my scheduled tax evaders should be an antiquarian."

"You can say that again!" George Mason replied. "But for him, the Potenti would still be in full swing and would have set Europe back at least fifty years with their reactionary agenda. But you must hold what I have just told you in complete confidence."

"You have my express word on that, Inspector," came the reply. "My father once told me, as a matter of interest, that one of their long-term aims was to restore the French monarchy, naming the Comte de Plesignac as claimant to the throne."

"In that event," remarked his astonished hearer, "they would have set Europe back even farther. France has been a republic for over two hundred years, apart from the royalist interlude under Napoleon the Third. I can take some small satisfaction in having frustrated their ambitions. *Feci quod potui*, as a matter of fact. I did what I could."

"You certainly did, Inspector," Leonard Parks affirmed, with a hearty laugh at his visitor's apt use of the society motto. "And you can take a great deal of credit for helping safeguard European democracy."

"Some of which I concede to my young colleague, Detective Sergeant Aubrey. She was most helpful at times when I was feeling rather stumped."

"I imagine those occasions were few and far between," the other generously allowed.

"Good of you to say so, in the circumstances," the detective replied, keenly aware that he had helped shatter a significant part of Leonard Parks' universe, with its links to previous generations of the aristocratic Farkas family.

"Have you booked the flight to England, Inspector?"

"Now that I know Dr. Weingarten is about to discharge you," the detective said, "I shall reserve seats on the flight from Kloten to Manchester Ringway, soon as I get back to Hotel Adler. That way, your wife Justine can drive down from Balderstones to meet us. I shall take the opportunity to visit my mother at Skipton, before returning by train to London."

"Very thoughtful of you, Inspector," Leonard Parks remarked. "I am keenly looking forward to it."

"*Feci quod potui*," Mason said, in his best Latin.

"*Faciant meliora potentes,* Inspector!"

"Let those who can do better!"

CPSIA information can be obtained
at www.ICGtesting.com
Printed in the USA
BVHW030200300119
539033BV00001B/15/P